Potomac Review

Potomac Review

Potomac Review is a journal of fiction, poetry, and nonfiction
published by the Paul Peck Humanities Institute at
Montgomery College, Rockville
51 Mannakee Street, Rockville, MD 20850

Potomac Review has been made possible through
the generosity of Montgomery College.

A special thanks to Dean Elizabeth Benton.

For submission guidelines and more information:
www.potomacreview.org

Potomac Review, Inc. is a not-for-profit 501 c(3) corp.
Member, Council of Literary Magazines & Presses
Indexed by the American Humanities Index
ISBN: 978-0-9990403-7-9
ISSN: 1073-1989

SUBSCRIBE TO POTOMAC REVIEW

One year at $24 (2 issues)
Two years at $36 (4 issues)
Sample copy order, $12 (single issue)

Table of Contents

Fiction

Anu Kandikuppa

HUMBUG 1

Joshua Jones

SOME MINOR COLLAPSE 13

Chloe Chun Seim

GODLESS 47

Mark Budman

HERE COMES THE SUN:
A REMASTERED *DIVUS* STORY 69

Mehdi M. Kashani

GOOD GIRL 91

Rahme Al-Mghayzawi, translated by Essam M. Al-Jassim

THE HOUSE NEXT DOOR 97

Azin Neishaboori

V LIKE VEGETABLE 105

Poetry

Jane Zwart

THE HOUSEHOLD GODS APOLOGIZE 11

Gloria g. Murray

MY FRIEND BECOMES A WARRIOR 31

Adam Day

FROM *MIDNIGHT'S TALKING LION AND THE WEDDING FIRE* 41

S. Shaw

EVERYTHING IS THE CROOKED MAN 65

RUNNING BLACK HOME 66

Mary Crow

CAPSIZED 71

IF YOU LOOK CLOSELY 72

SPRING FLOOD 74

Michael Kleber-Diggs

DISPATCH FROM MIDDLE AMERICA 87

EVERY MOURNING 88

MY ULTIMATE THOUGHT IS THIS 95

Julie Cadwallader Staub

LISTEN 100

SISTERS 102

Vernita Hall

BAIT BALL 116

ALIENATION 118

Nonfiction

Jane Hegstrom

A HOLY WAR 33

Richard Prins

THE LAPSED VEGETARIAN 77

Kate Carmody

FAMILY PIECE 121

CONTRIBUTORS 138

"How can you live with those pigeon feathers and pigeon poop?" they said.

Anu Kandikuppa

HUMBUG

A month after her husband Manu died, Bela got a phone call from Akash, whom she'd wanted to marry when she was nineteen. She was sitting by the window in her flat on the fourth floor of the family building and thinking about Manu when the phone rang. It was quiet without the clinking of his bottles and glasses. There was only the sound of the pigeons that flew in through the unbarred windows and fluttered about the room—the whir of their wings, their gurgles. "You can keep on living up there," Manu's brothers had said after the funeral and helpfully placed buckets under the biggest leaks in the roof to catch the rain. They kept living in the floors below and the family business kept running from the ground floor.

"Bela?" said Akash. "It's Akash. Akash Rao."

"Yes," said Bela, and before she could stop herself, "you too." She didn't care. If people couldn't excuse her in her present situation, when would they? She hadn't heard from Akash in fifteen years. People had been calling, but she hadn't expected him to call. She'd known who it was the second she heard the voice go boom-boom on the line, the way it had when he spoke to her in Economics class all those years ago. One look had been enough.

"Oh, Bela," said Akash. "It's so good to hear your voice!"

Not one but two wrinkles had formed on Bela's cheeks within the month—she was only thirty-four. She ran a finger down a wrinkle as if to erase it and pushed her lips out in a pout. She pulled a lock of hair out of her bun and wrapped it round and round her finger. She'd collected a number of odd habits over the years, like rare postage stamps, three or four a year. Now a pout, now a nervous titter, now a trailing off of words. The past month had been especially hard. The freedom was a bother – what to do with it? When she was growing up all the mothers on her street would warn their daughters, "Look at Bela. She never learns. Look how she cooks her own goose time and time again." Akash had ditched her fifteen years ago. Bela worked her lips nervously, in and out. She chewed them.

Luckily Akash talked so Bela didn't need to. Turned out he'd never married or even moved from their childhood town. Instead he'd done a Ph.D. in Oceanography and had lived this whole time with his sister, not far from Bela's old home. Bela wondered what it was like to graph an ocean. She imagined Akash on a boat – was he on one now? – pouring the ocean into little squares. Her stomach churned. She didn't like the ocean.

"It was because of you that I didn't marry, Bela," said Akash. He sounded hopeless and anxious, things he'd never sounded before. Bela eased up on her lips, but they were already raw. "I heard about your husband from the grapevine. I'm so sorry."

"Gripe vane?" said Bela. "What gripe v . . . ?" She tailed off.

"Hello? Hello?" said Akash. "It's really difficult to hear you, Bela. Maybe it's the connection? Do you still have the eyes? Oh, how I remember the eyes!"

Of course she still had the eyes, her enormous, liquid eyes – where would they go? Where had she learned how to wear a flirty look? She came from a conservative family. When she was very young her mother had taught her to sit with her legs crossed and her dupatta draped across her chest, but she forgot everything when she was with boys. She sometimes *did* think they were awful, their shirttails out, their toenails black with dirt, but mostly she couldn't do without them, the sweaty, loud creatures. How thrilled she'd been when they came to her like pins to a magnet! She had flaws. Her chest was flat, and so were her feet because of which she walked in a weird swaying way. But her eyes! They were such pools. Nothing else mattered. The other girls called her fast. The neighbors called her fast. Bela was delighted. She was a man-magnet. That's what she was.

She smiled happily.

What was this? Here she was, a grieving widow, cradling a phone to her cheek and smiling into it. That Akash! Still as glib as a weasel, if weasels were glib.

Bela erased her smile. "Of course I have my eyes," she said. "Two of them."

"Still can't hear you well," said Akash. "Maybe it's my mobile? Could you speak up, Bela? But I can imagine how devastated you must be."

Devastated. There was a good word. That's what she was, a young devastated widow. What a tragedy. Manu's liver had killed him, the naughty thing. Made him slump on the floor one night when she was taking him to bed. The doctors said he had months. Well, that was that with the marriage. Well, now there was no chance they could make it better. He'd already looked dead on the hospital bed, his lips curled back from his teeth, which had narrowed to points. She hadn't known how to comport herself after he died. No one would believe it if she cried. No one would believe she had loved him.

"Bela? Are you there? I don't think you have kids. That's what I heard anyway."

"No," said Bela. "Not a one. And you?"

"What? What did you say?"

"I said and you?"

She put out a hand. Tiny phantom fingers skimmed hers. She'd wanted children, of course, maybe they would keep Manu away from the drink? A good woman and some children, that was the answer. She would have been a good mother—she'd loved reading to Manu's nieces and nephews even though all they did was stare at her and fidget. Their mothers said it was because she read funny. "Funny, how?" Bela asked. Could she do nothing right? Funny, she stressed the wrong words and dragged out her syllables, they said. Funny, her voice was too sweet. She could tell they were suspicious. What was she after? Who could be sweet in her circumstances? They thought her sloppy. "How can you live with those pigeon feathers and pigeon poop?" they said. Why should they care? It all got cleaned up at some point.

But Akash was speaking. "How would I have kids, silly? I never married! At least it will be easier for you with no kids."

"Easier? For what?"

"Easier for you to find someone else?"

"Someone else?"

"I mean, uh," said Akash. His voice gathered strength. "I mean, I would love to see you, Bela. I want to see you."

Slowly Bela focused. Akash's face as she knew it floated into sight, except that he was bald. She could tell from his voice that he'd become bald. Bald people had deep voices while Manu had thick hair and a soft beautiful voice. But then Akash's voice had always been deep . . . Bela gave up.

Did Akash know about the money? Bela's eyes narrowed—she was impressed with her own shrewdness. Her mother said Manu's brothers owed her gobs of money for his share of the business and the building, which was worth crores in spite of the leaky roof and the pigeons. Even more if you considered she'd taken him off their hands by marrying him.

But there wasn't any money yet—and no one to ask. There was never anyone in the office when she peered through the glass, and her sisters-in-laws kept their curtains drawn and their children indoors. She had camped downstairs and waited for them. "In a few months," they said and helpfully picked up her grocery bags. "Soon," they said and hustled her up the stairs. Mrs. Khurana from the bookstore where Bela worked part time said she could stay with her as a paying guest in a room with a separate entrance and an attached bath. If she left the brothers would celebrate. Bela didn't want them to celebrate. She wasn't *that* silly. Besides, Manu wouldn't want them to celebrate.

"But you didn't want me," Bela said to Akash. "You said I was too clingy."

Silence.

"That's not fair, Bela. That was a long time ago," he said finally. "You don't know how I've kicked myself. You're not clingy, you're sweet and innocent and I realized it only later when I became more mature. Do you know, I'm close to tears right now because I'm talking to you?"

Did he know from the gripe van that Manu drank? Everyone knew. She too had known before they got married. Her mother told her. "I don't know, he's like a spare part in the family," she said. "Nobody cares what he does. But they're well-off. And you can't mope forever." Who would believe her if she said she'd seen something gentle and lost in Manu's eyes and known instantly that he was *her kind*? Not to mention his beautiful hands. Where else would she get such refined fingers and perfect oval nails?

"Bela, are you there?" said Akash, sounding impatient.

Anxious first, impatient second. Aha!

"Why do you keep falling silent? I know this is a lengthy call but it's important for you too. Living alone is hard, ask me about it, and you a woman. I really want to see you, Bela. Do you remember the first time we met, in Economics? Do you remember our looooong phone calls? Do you remember I kissed you one night? You liked me a lot, didn't you? What girl let a man kiss her in those days? Don't lie, I bet you remember!"

"I remember," said Bela, feeling weak.

She *did* remember the kiss in question, placed in the middle of her palm one night. She'd stolen out of her house to meet Akash so she could have a secret to hug to herself. She'd slipped her hand over the gate for him to nuzzle and felt in perfect tune with the handsome hunk, like she was playing a stringed instrument.

"Tell me what you remember," said Akash commandingly.

"You . . . um . . . my palm," said Bela.

"Was that your first kiss ever?" His voice was positively

deafening. "It's okay, we can say the k-word now. It's the twenty-first century. We were such idiots then, scared to touch because it would make a baby! Speaking of babies, there can be one now, Bela! Our baby! Do you feel shy when I say that? Do you?"

A cold draught wandered in and made Bela shiver. A pigeon stalked by her chair and cocked its head at her. She'd read that they were called "feral." She'd read that people put live wires on their windows to keep them out. When Akash had stopped talking to her she felt as if someone had reached inside her and scooped out everything that mattered. The sadness was a weight that pushed her into the earth. She couldn't take a single step. Her nostrils clogged up and her face swelled and snot flowed in rivers from her nostrils. "You aren't spicy enough," he'd said. What did it mean? Whatever it meant it meant she was easy to leave.

A second boy upped and left for New Delhi, a third two-timed her. The odd habits began. She smiled to herself and skulked in corners. She said "Hmmmmmmmmmmm" and pouted. "It's 22 point three two degrees Centigrade," she'd say. Or "Did you know that drug firms' prices have grown eye-poppingly large?" On occasion she roused herself and bought a new tube of lipstick or a necklace with green beads, but nothing was the same because she wasn't the same. She had been rewritten by boys. The other girls said, "It's her own fault." They didn't have Bela's eyes but they had things, good sense and street smartness, that mattered more.

"Hello? Hello? Have I lost you, Bela?" said Akash "I was talking about bab . . . "

"May 10th, 2004."

"What?"

"The last time you spoke to me."

"Oh, God, don't rub it in, Bela. I told you, I didn't know what I wanted. But I know now and it's you, Bela, only you. What must I do to make you believe me? But you remember the date, which means . . . "

"Akash . . . "

"Yes, Bela?"

"I think I've come to understand that . . . "

"What, Bela?"

"I must tell you that . . . "

"Hello? Hello? Curse this line! It's time I told you, Bela. I'm right outside your house! There! Are you excited? See, I cared enough to come all the way to see you. Paid Rs. 1,500 for the ticket. I'm coming up now, won't take no for an answer. I'm going to take care of you, Bela. I'm not going to be like that . . . like him."

Someone was stomping up the stairs. Someone pushed the door open. She never locked it anyway. With a rush of wings the pigeons flew about the room. "Understand what, Bela?" Akash said, waving his arms to ward them off. "Oh, there you are, my sweet Bela. You look exactly the same!"

If there was one thing Bela knew it was that she didn't look the same. She'd put on weight and was now the same shape as a Russian doll. It ran in the family. Her mother was perfectly round too.

Akash didn't look the same. He looked worn and respectable, tucked-in shirt, brown leather sandals. Bela was conscious of disappointment. Akash was bald and also had a paunch. She'd known from his voice he was going to be bald but she hadn't expected the paunch—there was no way you could tell that from a voice. His gaze flicked around the room, noting its size, noting the high ceilings, noting the vintage marble floors and the intricate fireplace. She knew that look.

"Understand that my Manu wasn't so bad—" she said.

It was true. Manu never made her cry. In fact it was his absence that made her cry. Manu hadn't cared about her funny faces and weird talk. He had given her presents and eaten whatever she made. Sure he drank, but that was because his family had let him. It was a hard habit to kick. They'd preyed on him and given him the flat with the leaky roof and taken his money. She recalled how, towards the end, he had become as light as a bird, had let her undress him down to his underpants and put him to bed. Her eyes misted over.

Akash sat down heavily. A pigeon pecked at his foot. He lunged at it.

"I know how happy you were together," he said. "But don't you want to move on to new things? I'd love to take you places, Bela. To Mauritius and the Andamans and . . . don't you want to travel? After living for fifteen years with that . . . "

"Akash . . . "

"Yes, Bela?"

"With what?"

"What?"

"Were you going to say something bad about Manu?"

"Of course not! Good man. I was going to say, with that good man. But why are you being so formal? May I approach you, Bela? May I hold your hand? You might have got up to greet me. I thought you'd be happier to see me but I understand. You're in mourning."

He knelt and took her hands in his, locked his eyes with hers and ran her bangles up and down her arm with a finger. Bela shivered. How many times had she imagined this? How many times had she dreamed of seeing Akash again, of touching him? Of riding behind him on his scooter, her hair flying, her arms around his waist?

"You hurt me," she muttered. "You made me cry."

"I know Bela, but that was then. I've settled down now. In spirit that is. Don't get me wrong, I'm open to quitting my job and moving here and helping you with your money—I mean your property matters. This is an expen—I mean nice house! And when everything is squared off we'll go everywhere, to Bali and Maldives and Seychelles. They're out of this world beautiful, Bela! I've been to all of them, to study the waves."

"Will we be near the water, Akash?"

"Yes, of course, silly! They are islands."

"Will we swim in the ocean?"

"Of course! All day if you like."

"Akash."

"Yes?"

"Do you remember when we went to Ramakrishna Beach with the whole class? And people were swimming and pulling other people into the water?"

"What? Yes, of course I remember. A wonderful trip. I remember you wearing a . . . a . . . you were so beautiful that day, Bela. You were so happy!"

"And this girl laughed and pulled me in and I screamed for you to help me but you said I mustn't be such a scaredy-cat and that even a child of two wouldn't cry? And I choked in the water and nearly drowned? And they had to rush me to the ER and I was there for two days and had to stay home and miss classes for a month?"

"Oh. Okay. I didn't remember that."

"I can't swim, Akash. I'm terribly afraid of water."

"Um, well, Bela, those are just details. We'll work out the details. We'll go to Switzerland or Austria instead. Heck, we'll stay right here if you like though we'll have to do something about these damn pigeons."

"Akash . . ."

"Yes, Bela?" He leaned in eagerly.

"I've had another thought . . ."

"Yes, yes, what is your thought?"

"I think that . . ."

"God, I thought it was the phone but it's you . . . you're mumbling. You always did. It's lack of confidence, that's what it is!"

"I've come to believe that . . . there's a word I'm thinking of but I can't remember it . . ."

"What? Just say it, damnit!"

"That it's all hubbub."

"What?"

"Humdrum."

"I fail to understand you, Bela. I've paid good money and come all this way to see you and you're just playing with me."

"Humbug. It's all humbug."

"What?"

"You're humbug."

From the window Bela watched Akash walk all the way down the street until he was a small dot and she couldn't see him anymore. On the mahogany wardrobe behind her, two pigeons lifted their rumps and went splat at the same time, a comforting sound. The sound of home.

Jane Zwart

THE HOUSEHOLD GODS APOLOGIZE

but none of us knows their tongue
and so we cannot tease the curses
from the benisons. With what
can we trust them?

Not with the child's milk teeth.
Nor with letters from our names.
We settle on a widowed earring
and a safety pin.

The fish dies, the roof leaks,
and the household gods apologize
or maybe they do not. Who are we
not to say amen anyway

to the silence they won't keep? Amen—
and reverse-engineer our prayers again
in the language our idols
eat but will not speak.

"I'm Alan," he said and immediately regretted it. He hated small talk.

Joshua Jones

SOME MINOR COLLAPSE

It was Alan's last day before retirement. He was fifty-three. With the latest round of furloughs and more cuts on the horizon, all Senior Analysts were out, and Gerry Pincus was in, sizing up Alan's office. He even brought a tape measure. Alan ignored him and continued filling a small cardboard box with the last of his personal effects. He paused at a signed photo of his old boss, from before she'd left for her Senate run. She was one of the good ones, so of course she lost, and Alan couldn't help thinking that all of this—the budget showdowns, the protests, the occupation on the Mall—it all might've been avoided had she gotten elected. He almost put the photo in his box and then he remembered: he'd heard she'd disappeared. He left it on the shelf.

"I thought you could see the White House from here," Pincus said, his nose smudged against the window, like a child waiting for snow, if the child was in his thirties and in a Brooks Brothers suit almost as shiny as his scalp.

"Only from the far corner," Alan said. It had a better view of the street below where, for the past few months, Alan had watched busloads of zombies unload and trickle south, toward the Mall. Sometimes they beat on drums. Once a few got arrested and hauled away in zip ties, to the Processing Centers, or so Pincus said.

Pincus grunted then asked if Alan was going to keep his plant, a browning ficus that'd been losing leaves for months now.

"Take it." Alan closed the box and taped it up. "I'm all done here."

They ducked out early and wound their way to F Street on their way to Paddy's Tavern and its overpriced drinks, but Pincus said he was buying, said he'd put it on his account—he was always bragging about his account—so Alan couldn't complain. Traffic was light. Only a small clump of zombies shambled southward with placards draped over their shoulders. "They've completely overrun the tidal basin," Pincus said. "Fucking leeches." Alan said nothing. His arms were tired from carrying his box, not that it was heavy. All it held was a half-empty bottle of bourbon; a stack of yellowed letters of commendation with inkjet signatures; a two-pack of floss, never opened; and a tube of KY Jelly, given by an anonymous prankster. *To help getting bent over less painful,* the attached note read. Lenny Gulman and David Burke got them too, but they were both past sixty and had checked out years before. Burke hadn't even bothered coming in for his last two weeks.

Now Gulman was waving to them from across the tavern. Paddy's was a small, dimly lit place, made up like some Old World pub with brass fixtures and vintage advertisements for beer they didn't sell. Gulman had secured a small table in the back with a circular bench. His hulking frame took up enough space for two. Beside him sat Marla in a cardigan that swallowed her, as if she were a burrowing mouse within its folds. Both their faces fell when they caught sight of Pincus.

"Burke couldn't make it?" Alan asked.

"Are you kidding? He hasn't left his house in days," Gulman said.

Alan was relieved they wouldn't have to make room for one more and sat beside Marla. Pincus made a show of asking what everyone was drinking and then disappeared to the front. Marla eyed Alan's box.

"That everything?" she asked.

"All that I felt like keeping. Everything else is in the trash."

"Over thirty years, and all you've got is a box of junk. Seems about right for this town," Gulman said.

"I hope you kept the KY," Marla said, her uneven smile jagging upward.

"And here I was thinking it was Pincus who gave those out," Alan said.

"Like he would ever think of that," she said. "He's a moron."

"I gave him my plant."

"He'll kill it if his thumb is as brown as his nose."

"He'll probably make Director in another year. Thank god I won't be around to witness that."

"Please, no. I'd have to shoot myself," Marla said.

"You don't want to do that," Gulman said. "It's the easiest suicide to screw up. Maybe a quarter of people can't even swallow a bullet correctly. You want to roll the dice with a one-in-four chance you'll be some drooling imbecile that has to have your diaper changed? I don't think so."

Pincus returned with a tray of shots and beer chasers and they toasted to early retirement and to furloughs and to fucking protesters and to getting out of this goddamned town. The tavern grew noisier and noisier until Gulman was shouting about the virtues of carbon monoxide and arguing against jumping in front of a metro train.

"But I don't have a car. Or a garage," Alan kept saying.

"You're not listening. The trains are never on time. *Never.* You'll screw it up."

"It's easy to do," Marla said with a wan smile. She had three attempts behind her — pills — from her "misspent youth," however long ago that was. Gulman liked to run and rerun numbers with her, to see what kind of dosage someone his size would need, but Marla's stockpile of Temazepam had expired, and they couldn't agree whether it'd be good enough to do the job. With all the shortages, who knew when she'd be able to get another refill.

"I'm telling you," Gulman continued, "monoxide is the way to go. Practically foolproof. And painless. You need to get yourself a car."

Alan nodded and nodded. The evening had dissolved into the swirling, smoky flavors of scotch and soda, and now his head felt heavy, inflated; the tavern air, stifling. "A car," Gulman repeated, but Alan was already leaving, pushing his way through the growing crowd.

The place had filled with the MBA set, all clones of Pincus. Alan sidled between a twenty-something shouting about repealing *posse comitatus* and another spiky-haired man shouting "pussy what?" over and over. They smelled of beer and canned body spray. Alan thought he might get sick until he finally reached the exit and pushed his way into the crispness of the October night.

The street was quiet but for the dull beat of drums coming from the Mall a few blocks away. A scent of ash hung in the air—the zombies had lit their fires again—and it was almost pleasant, bringing Alan back to long ago when he'd go camping on Assateague, back when there were still wild horses on the island. He and his friends would build a fire right there on the beach, spray themselves down with Off!, drink cheap beer, and watch stars emerge from behind windswept clouds. This was before grad school, before marriage, when there was no future beyond the scent of woodfire, of salt and sweat.

When he arrived at Metro Center, Alan remembered he'd left his box at the tavern. No matter. Only the bourbon was worth keeping, and even it was cheap and harsh and had to be drowned in soda. The thought of it made his head throb, and he wanted to sleep instead of waiting on the platform. Gulman was right. The train *was* terribly late. At least it stopped for him. He got onto one of the middle cars and settled into a torn vinyl seat that vaguely smelled of urine. He was almost the only passenger.

The train lurched forward and with it Alan's stomach. He took short, shallow breaths until the nausea passed. When he felt someone watching him, he straightened and tried to appear sober. He glanced down the aisle. His shoulders stiffened further. A zombie slouched a few seats away, looking straight ahead with those telltale vacant eyes and slack jaw. Alan wondered how it had slipped past security and why wasn't it at the Mall with the rest of them. He looked away, wishing he had a newspaper or anything he could pretend to read. Instead, he picked at his cuticles, peeled them back in a way that drove his wife crazy, before raising his eyes to see if the zombie had grown bored also. It stared right at him.

"Hi," Alan said. He didn't know why. He'd never talked to one. Never been so close to one.

The zombie's head pitched forward. A nod? Alan couldn't tell.

"I'm Alan," he said and immediately regretted it. He hated small talk.

The zombie just sat there, its head bobbing with the motion of the train. Perhaps it hadn't heard him. Alan returned to his nails and willed himself to keep his eyes lowered. He gnawed at a hangnail along his thumb until he tasted blood. When he looked up, he saw the zombie had moved seats and sat directly across from him. Alan let his hands fall in his lap. "Hi," he said again.

The zombie wore a rumpled suit with a greasy splotch the shape of a seagull across the lapels and grass stains on the knees. It had a damp, moldering smell and was slightly cross-eyed. Alan couldn't tell if it stared at him or something just past his left ear. Its shoulders slumped, its head also, and soon its limp jaw rested on its chest. Maybe it was tired of sleeping outside. Assuming it slept. The newscasts showed the zombies protesting at all hours, their incoherent chants and slogans punctured by the commands of the riot police. It was a sight to see, at first anyway. Alan was glad when the media turned their cameras elsewhere, to the earthquakes in Mexico, the California wildfires, the scandal with that *American Idol* singer.

His wife had fallen asleep again with the TV on, tuned into

one of her house shows that Alan pretended not to watch but secretly enjoyed. She was still in her scrubs, and Alan draped an afghan over her. On the screen, a too-tanned host swung a sledgehammer into a bank of kitchen cabinets that looked brand new. He was sure he'd seen the episode more than once, but he sat down by Joyce and turned the sound up. He didn't remember nodding off or relocating to their bed where he slept until the late morning sun woke him. Joyce had already left for work. She'd left a shopping list for him on the fridge with *p.s. Happy Retirement* at the bottom. Fresh fruit was on the list, and he had to walk an extra six blocks to find a store with anything other than canned goods. All that was left were apples, small and frost-bitten, but the grocer promised they were sweet. Alan bought as many pounds as he could carry and ate one on his way home.

As he walked, he realized he wasn't far from Dave Burke's place, a two-story colonial that once had a charming front garden but now was overgrown with a thicket of weeds. He tried the doorbell a few times but heard no chiming and then knocked until Burke shouted for him to come on in.

Inside smelled of nicotine and something fermented, but the living room looked much as Alan remembered it, from before, when Dave and his wife Lin hosted barbecues, summery affairs that Alan once dreaded but now seemed quaint. Burke always wore Hawaiian shirts and linen trousers to those. Now he was dressed in sweats and a bathrobe and had grown a food-stained beard. He offered Alan a beer and apologized that it wasn't cold. His block had been out of power for a week now.

"It's been the phone for Joyce and me," Alan said.

Burke opened his can of beer and sighed. "What can you do? Nothing. That's what."

"Gulman says I should get a car. For, you know, the carbon monoxide."

"Not a bad idea. Or you could drive to a bridge."

"I'm afraid of heights."

"For me, it's the falling. I think I could handle the impact, but that moment when you're in the air? With no control?" He held up his hand, hovered it in front of Alan's face as if it might plummet to the ground. His nails were chipped and bitten, far worse than Alan's, and yellowed from years of smoking. He lit a cigarette, apologetically, though Alan told him it was his own house and not to mind him. "Lin never let me smoke indoors," Burke said, and Alan tried to smile, as if this was a recurring punchline they shared, but Lin had been gone for over a year now. Disappeared. It happened in the first few months, when the news still covered the protests, when pundits declared they were on the brink of something, some minor collapse, some new normal that no one could agree on. Alan never did tell Burke that he thought he saw her, or something that looked like her, over a reporter's shoulder wielding a placard like a drum major's baton.

"Tell you what," Burke said, "if you get that car, take me for a spin. Lin would want me to get out. Out of this town. That was the plan, you know. Retire on the water. Wake up to the beach. That was the plan." He took a long drag on his cigarette then stubbed it out with a bony hand. He'd lost weight, Alan saw; his teeth were worse than ever.

"Sure," Alan said. "You can count on me."

That evening, Alan and Joyce carefully sliced the apples, pried the seeds from their hollows and pressed them into each other's palms, marveling at their symmetry. They placed the seeds in a cup and took small bites of the apple slices. They laughed at how good they tasted, the shriveled things, and slow danced across the rooftop deck. There were so few, but they made them last. Alan didn't tell her he left the largest bag with Burke. Below, the street was silent, black, the lamps long since extinguished. But even with the streetlamps out, there were no stars. Clouds hung heavy and orange above them with the promise of snow.

The trains came later and later. Alan graphed their arrivals and departures, used a stopwatch to calculate their speeds. He soon saw that Gulman was right, the trains were too unreliable, but he kept taking notes, riding the trains longer and longer each day, changing cars at each stop. It wasn't until he saw the zombie again that he realized he was looking for it.

It was on the Red Line wearing the same rumpled suit with the same seagull-shaped stain. Alan sat down across from it. It didn't acknowledge him, but kept its eyes fixed on a large poster advertising the new season of *Dancing with the Stars.*

"Hello again," Alan said.

The zombie blinked. Its mouth hinged shut little by little until its lips closed and it almost looked normal.

"Remember me? Alan?"

Its eyes slowly orbited to meet Alan's and blinked again. It seemed to straighten in its seat, or maybe Alan imagined it.

"I've been riding the trains too."

Yes, the zombie was definitely sitting straighter now. It had a thin, hollowed build that reminded Alan of the cancer patients Joyce sometimes tended. The folds of skin beneath its eyes were heavy and swollen. It needed a shave.

"I've been taking notes for a friend. Well, not a friend, but colleague. Former colleague. I don't suppose you'd know about that."

More blinking. Faster now.

"What am I talking about. Of course you would. Anyway, he thinks I should get a car."

The zombie leaned forward. A security badge slipped from its jacket, dangling from a nylon lanyard. There was a government seal, a photo, a name.

"Your name's Fahd? Am I saying that right?"

Blinking again. A dip and rise of the head.

The train braked and eased to a stop and the doors hissed open. "This is my stop," Alan said. Fahd remained motionless as Alan exited the car. The platform was deserted. The overhead fluorescents flickered and hummed. Alan stepped on the escalator and shot a backward glance to the zombie, now standing in the train's doorway. Its eyes followed Alan as he floated along the escalator toward the surface.

It was past two a.m. when the car alarm went off, disorienting Alan, transporting him to a time when the street was full, when garbage trucks clipped the shittily parked Hyundai at the end of the block. He got out of bed and padded to the window. Below him, a car sat angled halfway in the street with its door open, as if the driver, in the middle of parking, said to hell with it and walked away. Its hazards pulsed on and off, bathing the street in their amber glow. Alan watched and waited, but no neighbor—how many were even left now?—came to shut off the alarm.

The next morning Gulman answered his door red-faced and sweating and coated in sheetrock dust. Tools were scattered across his living room. "Scaffold," he explained, and showed Alan his handiwork: the drywall and joists above the doorway to his bedroom had been cut away. In the opening, he'd wedged a metal chin-up bar. "Amazon still delivers, you know," Gulman said. "And it's rated for 500 pounds, so I should be good."

"What about the monoxide route?"

"You going to get a car?"

"Already got one."

Gulman's eyes widened. He pushed past Alan and waddled to his balcony. "Which one?"

"The green one. Over there."

"Alan. Jesus. That's a Prius."

"But it was free."

"It's a fucking hybrid."

"It has a tailpipe. I just thought—"

"You just thought. Give me a hand with the rope while you're here. Know how to tie a noose?"

"I can tie a slip knot."

"Jesus."

"I'm sure I could learn."

"Forget it," Gulman said. He leaned heavily against the balcony. Looked like he might pitch over the edge. "Who's that in the car?" he asked.

"Nobody. Just someone I met. His name's Fahd."

Burke's door was wide open. A skinny cat sat in the middle of the room, bathing. Alan couldn't remember Burke having a cat, was sure that Burke hated cats. "Burke?" he called. His voice echoed harshly off the vacant walls. Behind him shuffled Fahd, even though Alan told him to stay in the car. He still hadn't told Joyce about him. About how he found him lurking along their street when he went to turn off the car alarm, even though he told Joyce it would go off on its own. And it did. He'd gone outside in the cold in nothing but pajamas and an old pair of sneakers for nothing. By the time he reached the car, its alarm had gone quiet. He wasn't surprised to see the keys still inside it; he knew its owner wouldn't be back. It was after he'd eased the car out of the middle of the street and was trying to remember how to parallel park that he caught sight of the zombie in the headlights. Alan let out a cry and jammed his foot down. The car lurched forward before Alan found the brakes and stopped inches from Fahd's shins. Fahd stared into the halogen beams unblinking, his mouth almost a perfect O and letting out bright plumes of breath. If the zombie was cold, he didn't show it.

Now Fahd stutter-stepped into Burke's living room, sniffed the air, and made his way to the sofa where he sank into its oversized cushions. The cat paused its bathing to rub against Fahd's legs before jumping into his lap. It let out a soft meow and began kneading Fahd's thighs with its paws. Fahd blinked at the animal and lifted a hand as if to pet it. His palm fell heavily, cuffing the cat hard on the back, but the cat didn't seem to mind.

Alan wandered through dusty rooms, past unwashed dishes and piles of musty laundry, until he reached the master suite. There, the bed lay stripped of its bedding, and the bare mattress had two human-sized depressions, one smaller than the other. On the bedside table sat a brass-framed photo of Burke and his wife, each of them with forced smiles, a crowded ballroom behind them. From one of the embassy open houses. Alan and Joyce had gone too. This was during the previous administration, before Lin's cancer scare, back when Burke still had hair. Alan tried to remember which embassy but couldn't. Not that it mattered. Most of them had closed months ago.

Alan returned to the living room just in time to hear a muffled cry followed by a flash of fur darting out the front door. Fahd had sunk deeper into the couch cushions, and now he was touching his face over and over and moaning softly. A scratch ran from below his eye to the corner of his mouth and wept a steady trickle of blood. Alan found some paper towels and dabbed at Fahd's cheek. "You've got to be more careful," he said. "You've got to be gentle with animals." Fahd blinked and worked his mouth into a strange rictus. A smile, Alan realized.

"It can't stay here," Joyce said.

"He has nowhere to go."

"Take it to the Mall. Or wherever they're putting them these days. You can't be serious."

Fahd stood in the corner of their kitchen, staring into their back garden. It was a bad year for Joyce's plantings. Her hydrangea, once bursting with pink blooms, now drooped and was coated in a light snow, the first of the season.

"It's cold," Alan said.

"It stinks."

Alan nodded. He'd driven back from Burke's with the windows all the way down. "Maybe we can give him a bath."

"It's not a dog."

"No. It's—I mean *he's*—not," Alan said. He didn't mention how Fahd hung his head out the car window and grinned his crazy leer as the first flakes of snow swirled about them. "Just a bath. Or shower?" he said. "Joyce, please. He's harmless."

"I'm not helping you. Don't expect me to wash his clothes!"

Fahd leaned his head against the Prius's window, his hair still wet and smelling of Joyce's conditioner. Alan's suit was too big for him, but at least it didn't reek of subway musk. Joyce said they should throw out Fahd's old one, but Alan said he knew of a dry cleaner still open, down the road from Gulman's place. And with the streets so empty now, it'd take no time at all. Even so, he drove slowly and favored side streets to avoid the checkpoints. Not that having Fahd with him was a crime, not exactly, but he'd heard reports of round-ups, of the creation of special courts, or so Pincus claimed—but Pincus was always bragging about his Homeland Security contacts. The side streets were empty. No police cruisers, no black SUVs with tinted windows, not even pedestrians. It wasn't until he turned onto Gulman's block that he saw someone, a woman, her hand clamped against her forehead and blood running down her temple.

He jammed his foot on the brake. Fahd scissored forward, his face hitting the dash with a fleshy thud, but Alan was already out of the car and running. "Marla!" he called. "Marla!"

She staggered and slumped to the sidewalk. "Alan?" she said, and then, "He did it. He finally did it." A sobbing noise burst from her, or maybe a laugh, it was hard to say. Alan helped her to her feet. She was lighter than she looked. Weightless, almost. "I can manage," she kept saying, but she clung to his arm and let him lead her to the car where Fahd sat, no longer slumped over in the seat.

Fahd turned to stare at them. His large nose was bent, and blood streamed from both nostrils and spattered over Alan's shirt, an old Oxford that no longer fit him, but still . . .

"Jesus," Alan said. "The sight of you two." He used one of his old handkerchiefs to staunch their wounds, Marla's first. He daubed at her head, and she spoke rapidly about what happened, about how Gulman had gotten in touch with her, had been trying to call her for days but with the phone outages he'd had to track her down in person, walking much of the way, and she thought he was going to have a heart attack then and there.

"Look up," Alan instructed. He peered at her cut. It wasn't as bad as he first thought; the blood was already forming a dry ridge in her hair.

"He said he didn't want to do it alone. So I said yes. I kept thinking he'd change his mind. We finished off that bottle of scotch he always talked about, then I helped him onto the chair." She paused and squinted at Fahd who had stuck a finger up each nostril. Alan handed him his handkerchief and told him to use that instead. "He wobbled a bit and he wanted me to hold his hand. When he stepped off, something must've gone wrong because the whole thing came down. The bar, I mean. It hit me, and I don't know, I passed out? Blacked out? I don't remember coming outside at all. But Gulman. I remember him lying there. He didn't cry out or anything. It must've been instant just like he wanted. I think it was instant." Her voice trailed off, and she stared hard at Fahd. "Who's that?"

"Come on," Alan said. "Let's check on Gulman, make sure he's dead. And see if he has a first aid kit."

Gulman had cleaned up since Alan last visited: vacuumed; dusted; a lemony scent of furniture polish filled the small space. The windows were open and the chill from outside filled the living room, the kitchen, the hallway. And there, at the end of the hall, lay a pair of thick legs splayed across the floor, unmoving.

"Wait," Alan said. "Let's find that first aid kit." Under Gulman's sink, he found gauze bandages and alcohol swabs. Marla winced as he cleaned her wound. Her eyes kept flicking up toward Fahd as if trying to piece together who, or what, he was. Or maybe she knew already. She must know. Wasn't her ex-wife one of the first, back when they thought the protests were temporary? As for Fahd, he held a wad of toilet paper to his nose and grinned at his reflection in the bathroom mirror.

"I didn't think he'd go through with it," Marla said as Alan finished bandaging her head. "But he's happy now. Right?"

Alan shot a nervous glance toward the stumpy feet down the hall. Gulman had his best loafers on, freshly polished and gleaming.

"Maybe we should cover him?" she said. She took Alan's hand and pulled him down the hall. Fahd shuffled behind, still holding the tissues to his nose though his bleeding had stopped. There Gulman lay, his arms stretched overhead like he was announcing a touchdown. He wore his best suit, had even worn his diamond-studded tie-pin. The noose was snug about his neck but didn't look too tight. It was still wrapped around the chin-up bar that lay on the floor beside him, one end wet with blood from where it'd struck Marla. There was no sign of head trauma on Gulman at all. Instead, he looked restful, almost like he was sleeping. It was then that Alan saw it, the gentle rise and fall of Gulman's belly. The legs twitched, and Gulman opened his eyes.

"What are you all doing here?" he said and rubbed the back of his head. Then, peering at Fahd, said, "What the fuck is that *thing* doing here?"

"His name is Fahd," Alan said.

"It's a goddamn zom—"

"I said, his name is Fahd."

"Get it out of my home," Gulman said, trying to rise. Alan and Marla each took an arm and pulled, but Gulman's frame sagged; his feet wouldn't stay underneath him. They all grunted as Gulman planted his feet and tried again, but his body barely got an inch off the ground before he collapsed, panting, his face reddening. Sweat beaded across his forehead. He looked as if he might cry.

Marla knelt beside him and caressed his arm. Alan paced the bedroom, taking in Gulman's framed movie posters—*Bullet* and *Dirty Harry*, *Serpico* and *The Deer Hunter*. It was then that Fahd stepped forward, took both of Gulman's hands and pulled the large man to his feet as if he were nothing more than a large sack of groceries.

"Let go of me, you freak," Gulman sputtered and shook off Fahd's grip. Fahd's rictus grin dropped and his jaw fell slack. His gaze drifted to the faces in the posters, finally resting on the one of De Niro holding a gun to his head, the actor's haggard eyes not unlike Gulman's.

"You hurt his feelings," Alan said.

"Feelings?" Gulman's hands shook. He tugged at the noose, at the chin-up bar still tethered to the other end of the rope. He worked the rope off his neck and pointed at Fahd with the bar and shook it. "What does this thing know about feelings?" He raised the bar high. His eyes bulged. His jaw quivered. He stood like that, arm suspended, trembling, until Alan said, "Let's go, Fahd." Then his arm dropped, and the chin-up bar clattered to the floor.

Gulman let out a single choked sob and his shoulders heaved up and down. Marla patted him on his back, but he waved her off. "Just go," he said, his voice almost a whisper.

Fahd rode in the backseat, clutching the dry-cleaning ticket like Alan told him to. Marla sat in the front, studying Fahd, his crooked nose, the way he stared out the window.

"It has sad eyes," she murmured. "Will you take it to the Mall?"

"Joyce said I should."

"But you're not going to."

"No."

"Good."

They drove in silence. Fahd pressed his face to the window as they passed Rock Creek Park. Its thick screen of trees was black against the backdrop of melting snow and the remnants of the encampments—shredded tarps, an overturned port-a-john, a stack of partially burnt mattresses. Burke used to jog here, was always trying to get Alan to join him. Alan half expected to see him now, shambling among the wreckage and the trees.

"Burke's gone." He breathed out the words, more to himself than to Marla.

"Disappeared?"

"I got the car for him, you know. He wanted me to take him for a spin. He wanted to go to the beach. To retire there. With Lin."

"I'm so sorry."

"I haven't been to the beach in years."

"Do you think it's still there? I mean, everything's disappearing now. It's still there, isn't it?"

The Bay Bridge was empty, and Alan slowed as he reached its apex trying to calculate the distance to the water below. He would have to ask Gulman about it. Beside him, Joyce scanned the Chesapeake. She'd taken one look at Marla and Fahd's injuries and insisted on coming. "You don't want to fool around with head injuries," she'd said. Then, looking at Alan, "Besides, somebody has to organize things." She had them fill up a cooler, had them pack blankets, matches, extra clothes, saying, "You never know." She was always the pragmatic one, but there was something giddy in her movements, something they all felt as they got on the highway and the city fell away behind them.

Marla slept in the back seat, nestled up against Fahd's shoulder, and he laid his hand on her head, his fingers gently tracing the scar at her temple. Joyce had set and bandaged his broken nose, leaving him looking like a deranged rhinoplasty patient.

Now Fahd's eyes stared across the flattened landscape of the Eastern Shore as they passed boarded up restaurants and deserted fruit stands and acre after acre of empty farmland. There were hardly any other cars. It wasn't until they neared a former chicken plant that they saw distant figures moving beyond a fence line topped with razor wire. The figures were dark and shadowy against the whitewashed chicken coops, and Alan saw that they shambled. He was glad Fahd was looking out the other window, his eyes transfixed by the barren fields.

They drove on. Gulls replaced crows. It wasn't long before they smelled the ocean. They saw a makeshift barrier stating the National Seashore was closed due to lack of funds and violators would be prosecuted, but there were no signs of rangers or police. Large swaths of the road were covered in sand, the parking lot too, as if the surrounding dunes were reclaiming what was theirs. How much longer till the sea oats took root, till the salt and sea air turned the asphalt to a fine gravel? Till the wild horses came back?

The tang of the ocean filled Alan's lungs as he trotted up the dunes behind Joyce. She'd taken off her shoes, and Alan saw that she still painted her toenails. Why hadn't he noticed that before? She wriggled her feet in the sand and laughed. "It feels good," she said. The wind whipped her voice about, making her sound young, a girl even. Alan tugged at his shoes, his socks. The sand was cold, but the grit did feel good. He rolled up his pants legs and followed Joyce toward the surf.

Behind him, Fahd lumbered across the dunes, almost loping, and Marla beside him holding her sandals. Plovers ran in and out of the surf. An egret eyed Fahd curiously before flying away at his approach. He neared the tide-line and jumped as a foamy tongue surged toward him, then he let out a harsh barking noise—a laugh—and let the tide rush over his shoes, soaking the legs of his trousers. He bark-laughed with each spray of water, and Alan, Joyce, and Marla joined him, each of them shrieking with delight whenever the icy surf lapped at their bare feet. Their shadows stretched out long in front of them. The water glowed pink in the dusky light.

They built a fire from driftwood and scattered trash. There would be fires that night on the Mall, Alan knew. They'd been building them higher and higher, but nobody cared anymore. It was only a matter of time before they spread. Fahd ran up and down the beach looking for more fuel. Marla sat huddled next to Joyce, her eyes damp, from the wind or the smoke, Alan couldn't tell.

"Do you think they'll ever come back?" she asked.

"They say they swam away," Joyce said. "I like to think they're still out there, swimming somewhere."

Alan said nothing. He watched Fahd trotting down the beach and dragging a gnarled limb. In the fading light, it looked like a long, twisted bone. The sun had fallen below the horizon, and everything looked skeletal and bleached. Bluish white. Like ghost horses crashing through the waves. Fahd threw the branch on the fire. Sparks shot upward, curled in the air with the smoke.

They would return to the city tomorrow, Alan knew, but for now he inhaled the scent of the flames and the saline air. It was a moonless, cloudless night, and stars netted the sky. They looked different to Alan, as if someone had rearranged the constellations when he wasn't looking. But they hadn't disappeared, not yet.

MY FRIEND BECOMES A WARRIOR

(for Lynn & Lauren)

while her daughter lies in the hospital O.R.
after having part of her liver excised
my friend becomes a warrior

stands with spear in hand
stands like an Amazon woman, ready to battle
armies of invaders, who would dare
to take her daughter from her

she strikes out, piercing the tip of her spear
into every one of them and she will not stop
until she has saved her daughter, even if
she should lose her own life—she will not stop

my friend has become a warrior
with a war cry so loud it echoes down
the hospital corridors, through the sealed door
over the surgeon's sterile gloves and straight
into her daughter's heart

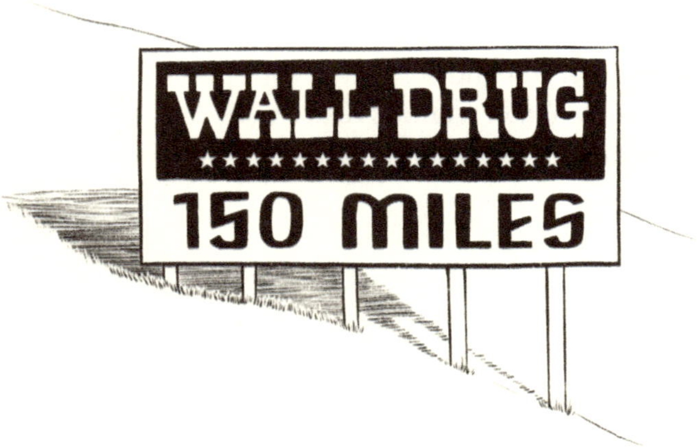

My family climbed out of our car and walked up to Wall Drug Store, where two teepees were set up.

JANE HEGSTROM

A HOLY WAR

If you happen to be driving through the Midwest on your way to see Mount Rushmore in the Black Hills of South Dakota, I would encourage you to take the time to turn off the highway and experience a quintessential midwestern small town—my hometown. You will find several lovely churches, neat tree-lined streets, parks, corner groceries, and the ghost of a small downtown. As in thousands of other small towns across America, the businesses that were on Main Street have relocated to highways on the outskirts of town. Those highways will take you past strip malls with names like Peddler's Village, Shops of Camelot, or Harbor Centre (never mind that the closest body of water is a hundred miles away). The new "main streets" are now monotonous gray ribbons of highways that disappear into distant mirages.

Midwesterners are an unpretentious people who work hard, are polite, and are ready to help strangers. Drivers are especially courteous and road rage unthinkable. In fact, midwestern men will wave to you from their cars, a salutation called a "finger wave." With a finger wave, the driver's hand never leaves the steering wheel, but the index finger points straight up and wags back and forth. The friendliest men will also give you a slight nod as they finger wave past you. And if you need assistance locating a residence, be prepared for detailed directions that involve taking a sharp left turn at the corner where there is a house with a large birdbath in the front yard and the place you are looking for is the gray house next door with the red jeep parked in the driveway.

If you have time to chat with midwesterners, you will find

their conversations sprinkled with words like please, thank you, you betcha, and ah geez. And you never have to worry about them bringing up uncomfortable topics of conversations. But be warned, you will render them speechless if you share personal information.

Growing up where nearly everyone is united by a common cultural heritage isn't something a person thinks about. It's taken for granted—a warm, safe, undemanding way of life. And cultural homogeneity presumes there will be less conflict when nearly everyone has the same political ideology, is in the same socioeconomic class, and shares a common appearance.

Today, like most midwesterners, South Dakotans are generally politically conservative people who belong to the Republican Party. In fact, the Republican Party originated in the Midwest in the mid-1850s and, at the time, was against white southerners and Catholic immigrants. And the Republican Party has carried the state's electoral votes in all but five presidential elections; a famous outlier was George McGovern, the Democratic nominee for the presidency in 1972. A Democrat has not won the governorship since 1974, and Republicans hold large majorities in both the state house and senate.

Midwesterners are also largely middle class, the majority being shopkeepers and farmers. Long after I left South Dakota, I realized that the alley across the street from my childhood home offered a glimpse into the backstage lives of families, an early education in class and income differences. Two houses stood out from all the rest; they were doctors' houses, both more beautiful than any of the others. One was a large, dark brick house and the other a gray contemporary design, strangely out of place in that prairie locale. Doctors and lawyers, with their university degrees and beautiful homes, were viewed as different—as "other," a curiosity. Townspeople and farmers were always cordial, polite, and appreciative of their skills but, as Kathleen Norris wrote in her book *Dakota: A Spiritual Geography*, midwesterners "seem to have a collective inferiority complex that views doctors and lawyers with suspicion because, after all, if they practice here, they can't be all that competent."

The Midwest is typically seen as a racially homogeneous region settled by people of northern European descent. German Americans are the largest ancestry group in addition to a large Scandinavian-descended population. And it's true that midwestern states occupy prominent positions in the category of the top ten whitest states; my home state of South Dakota is number 10.

In 1955, South Dakotans of Native American and Alaska Native ancestry were only 3.6 percent of the population. But given that two of the nine Native American reservations in South Dakota were in close proximity to my hometown, I find it inexplicable that I never saw a Native American until that year, when I was eleven and hundreds of miles away.

It was the month of July, and my parents, four siblings, and I were in a hot, overstuffed car headed for the western part of the state to visit my grandparents. Our gas was running low when we drove into Wall, the mother of all tourist-trap towns, to fill up the tank.

Wall's claim to fame has always been Wall Drug Store, a seventy-six-thousand-square-foot emporium with, among other attractions, a movie theater, arts and crafts stores, a statue of a jackalope (and many jackalope items for sale), and a life-size cement dinosaur. Even today, their famous free cups of ice water and five-cent coffee are advertised on billboards that paper the interstate from Minnesota to Montana. In his book *The Lost Continent*, Bill Bryson wrote that Wall is "an awful place, one of the world's worst tourist traps, but I loved it and I won't have a word said against it."

My family climbed out of our car and walked up to Wall Drug

Store, where two teepees were set up. Native American men sat in front of them, wearing moccasins and rawhide pants. A couple had feathered headdresses. On the tables before them, handmade goods like bead-worked necklaces, toy drums, peace pipes, knife sheaths, and tomahawks were laid out for sale. I remember trying hard not to stare at the men with their long, braided hair and thinking that must be how all Native Americans dressed and the way they led their lives on reservations.

James Shortridge, a cultural geographer whose focus has been primarily on the Midwest, has written that Native American Indians constitute an important part of the overall "western" flavor that most of the popular literature gives to South Dakota. This flavor is rooted in tourism: buffalo herds, caves, patriotism, mines, rodeos, mountain scenery, and the badlands. The uniting theme is "where the West still lives." But what I learned over time was that for Native Americans, the colorful theme belied the reality of poverty, poor nutrition, and, according to the U.S. Department of Health and Human Services, in 2017 the infant mortality rate for American Indians/Alaska natives was twice that of non-Hispanic whites—American Indian /Alaska natives (9.2) and non-Hispanic whites (4.7).

High on a shelf in the guest bedroom closet, I have an old hatbox decorated with orange, maroon, green, and brown flowers. It holds black and white photographs dating back to my early childhood—of my younger siblings, Christmases, Easters, picnics at the lake, even a picture of a picnic in a cemetery. One picture is of me wearing jeans and a white T-shirt, both hands firmly on the grips of my new, blue, birthday bicycle. When I look at that photo, I'm a third grader again in the waning days of May, awaiting the first thrilling days of summer right around the corner.

In the alley across the street from my house, the Brogan brothers were playing catch. Slipping my baseball glove through the handlebars, I pushed my bike as fast as I could, bounced onto the seat, and pedaled with all my might until, about ten feet from the boys, I slammed on the brakes, causing my bike to spin into a full circle, theatrically spraying gravel at their feet.

"Hi!" I said. "You guys need a third person to play catch?"

"No," Jimmy Brogan said.

"Why not?" I asked.

Looking at his brother Johnny, Jimmy sneeringly said, "Because you can't catch my fast balls. And besides that, you don't belong to the one true church."

Most boys Jimmy's age have a gawky look about them—unbearably skinny bodies with dangling arms and legs that appear too uncoordinated to even support a run to first base. But Jimmy was different. He was tall for his age and extremely coordinated with brownish-blonde hair and blue eyes that at times flashed a steel gray.

Jimmy had a look on his face that I'd never seen before. He didn't look mad; it was more a mean look, or maybe disgust. What had I done? We'd always been pals. Well, as much as it was possible for an eleven-year-old boy and a nine-year-old girl to be pals. Sure, given the choice, he'd rather play with the boys, but he seemed okay playing with me too. Why, just the night before we'd been on the same team playing ante-I-over. I never threw a pigtail, and we ended up winning. And in the winter the boys let me play crack-the-whip at the neighborhood ice-skating rink.

"One true church?" I asked in surprise. "Whaddya talking about, one true church?"

"The Catholic Church is the one true church. It started way before your church. It's been around lots longer, that's why it's the one true church," Jimmy repeated, "and you're going to hell because you don't belong to the one true church."

I belonged to the First United Methodist Church, but I didn't know its age. Only later did I learn that Jimmy was correct: John Wesley, the founder of Methodism, was born in 1703, but the

Catholic Church claimed its beginnings seventeen hundred years before that.

Then, with what seemed to come out of nowhere, I snapped back, "I wouldn't want to be a Catholic, because you worship the pope—not God. And besides that, you confess your sins to a priest, and he forgives your sins. That's wrong! Only God can forgive sins." Jimmy quickly countered that priests worked like a channel to God to hear and forgive sins. My comeback was that when Protestants confess their sins, they do it directly to God; no intermediaries for us. And besides that, Catholics play bingo, and gambling is a sin.

Ignoring my bingo argument, Jimmy shot back that Protestants don't understand sin and that I had no idea about all the different sins.

"Yes, I do!" I said.

Snickering, Jimmy said, "Oh yeah, tell me what a mortal sin is."

"Mortal sin?" I asked.

"See!" Jimmy said, "I told you. You don't know nothing about sin. A mortal sin is the worst! You go to hell for a mortal sin. It's like if you don't go to church or you murder someone."

Then, tucking his thumb into the loop of his jeans and puffing his chest out, Jimmy said, "And then there's venial sin."

Confused, I asked, "Venial sin?"

"Yeah!" Jimmy continued. "See, how can you ask God to forgive your sins when you don't even know about all them different sins? Heck, you probably don't even know when you're sinning. But I'll tell you about venial sins. They aren't as bad as mortal sins. It's stuff like not cleaning up your room when your mom and dad ask you to and complaining about it."

"But you believe that babies that die and aren't baptized go to limbo. That can't be!" I shot back. "Babies that don't get baptized haven't done anything wrong. They haven't done any sins. Why wouldn't they go straight to heaven?"

Jimmy's smug response was, "Because of the original sin. When Eve gave the apple to Adam in the Garden of Eden, that made everyone sinners. It was the original sin, the first sin. Get it? That's why you get baptized, to get cleared of the original sin. But babies that die before they get baptized still have the original sin hanging onto them, so they don't get to go to heaven or hell, they just go to limbo."

It was then, in my alley, when I first understood that other churches had beliefs different from mine. And the differences between our churches were more than Catholics playing bingo and eating fish on Fridays. It was more than praying to Mary and muttering over each well-worn rosary bead, or priests and nuns dressed in black. There were different sins.

Jimmy was right. I had no idea that a sin was anything but a sin. And I admit that I marveled at how organized Catholics were with the way they sorted out every sin and put them into neat groups.

Little has changed in the lives of Catholics and Protestants in my hometown, and I imagine elsewhere for that matter, where tacit agreement on religious segregation in certain areas of life has endured. In many American towns there are separate cemeteries for Catholics and Protestants. And although today there are conflicting opinions as to whether Catholics are forbidden to join the Masonry, when I was young it was clear: Catholics who became Masons had sinned and couldn't receive Holy Communion.

In my hometown, the most obvious form of segregation was the education system. Catholic schooling generally ended in the ninth grade, necessitating attendance at the public high school from the tenth grade to graduation. There are no words to adequately describe the tenth-grade public school girls' heart-stopping thrill when Catholic boys were seen roaming the halls for the first time. I remember thinking that the addition of Catholic boys was like a caravan of new, beautiful beings that entered our world. And I choose to think that Catholic boys and girls looked at the public school boys and girls in the same way.

I've come to believe that no matter how homogeneous a culture is, people will look for differences—look hard and even insist upon finding them. Uncovering differences seems to be a primordial force, a need to unearth something to squabble about, a desire to create comparisons that will inevitably lead to division and conflict. At the age of ten, I had stumbled upon an ancient conflict—a holy war—only this one was between me and my playmate.

The standoff between Jimmy Brogan and me persisted for much of the summer. There were never any stones thrown, no hitting, shoving, or slugfests; our parents wouldn't have allowed that. But something had changed. There was a tiptoeing about, a feeling of being on high alert, the expectation of an insult, a slight. The carefree casualness of being neighborhood playmates was over. I had fewer calls to join the Brogan boys to play kick the can or red rover and, slowly, we left each other for our own kind—reaching out and away from our neighborhood and into the world.

ADAM DAY

FROM *MIDNIGHT'S TALKING LION AND THE WEDDING FIRE*

"Pursuing medicine at community level" might be link between
troubled mind and lived environment, the pathogenic agency
of an individual's social and material context. Instead
of seeking internal cause of mental illness, in either
unconscious mind or damaged brain, look to external realities—
ethnic and racial discrimination and poverty. Profile Puerto

Rican immigrant youth gang member convicted of murder, which
suggested "ruthlessly hostile environment" of upbringing U.S.,
abroad as much to blame as anything for psychological distress,
criminal behavior. 'What else, else could one expect? People
packed—1600 to the acre—into filthy, decaying tenements."
Ellison picked up this arguing "slum scenes of filth, disorder,
and crumbling masonry "were severely "damaging to Negro
personality." ______ was not just a ruin, in other words, but
also a pathogenic agent America, elsewhere. This lived
environment understanding Ellison meant to explore, resist
as he sat down to work the Invisible.

Had he believed identity anywhere if fixed in this manner,
would not have been able to make argument demonstrating
how the pressure of certain environment, the urban North,
fuels "desperate search for identity" among black Americans.
A dynamic interplay between self and site, identity
and environment. Indeed, the moment an "inmate" enters
asylumjailschoolmilitary "he begins a series of abasements,
degradations, humiliations, and profanations of self," precisely
because such sites are "forcing houses for changing persons,"
the site itself set up to remake the self.

"To re-forge the will to perform "each bewildered patient" sees "into the friction between "his problems and his environment" to see that "the young" are educated to fulfill the purpose of the educated to fulfill other words. Give me the young for the rest of his or her life questioning why, as a platform for spying up.

Given conditions, how does detainee, sectarian/partisan or invalid "stripped" of "civilian self" manage to assert individuality; question takes granted persistence of individual agency in face of adverse social strictures—-regation, -crimination, -ercion—point Ellison made throughout career whenever he noted, the "willful, complexly compelling human" facts within and against "the divisions of [his] society."

So asks how is writing supposed to respond to the faithful but inevitably flawed? Mogadishu, Sandy Hook, Garissa: Enacts it? Totalization of returning to the same piece each day, which covers, reveals and alters one to the next, providing context and limitation at door which was crying, and said "Don´t cry, we were living fear, but now will live hope" (- Tristan Bernard).

The inability of narrative to explain the effect the self-iterative, and such possible impossibility of forging an or relationship with the other to use breaches that provide enticing resistance while inviting participation, creating art in the context of gaps lives in wilder copies which is great contractions and
the faceless use their eyes to steel see do it distorted and you
a million of you in flames.

Not reading another poem like water tastes. Believes and yet questions poetry language: might make anything become? Performative utterance "setting the thing named apart from all else." Language haunt. And in that vein, forget. Forget. "What do [poems] have to talk about [?]." What do they have? Against the balance of navel-revelatory reproductions? Tongue-in-cheek.

Obviously, often the world makes only some sense, so why expect easily "unfurled tongues that won't mouth, mass swerving from the law." If catharsis or revelation: usually what we already know we don't entirely understand, puzzles to some, might genuine history tenor. Accumulative stresses & limit tone think, a measure of others to the extent that is ever. Tired of waiting till they understand. See you/it later.

He pressed the cool pop can to my arm. Again and again.

Chloe Chun Seim

GODLESS

It was a high distinction to be a farm girl in central Kansas. You knew the country. Your blood—or if not yours, your ancestors'—had been poured into the soil. Had enriched it. Our family, the Wells family, had offered substantial sacrifice through our five decades on this farm. A young boy, my uncle. Three of my unborn siblings, come into this world through so much pain the woods to the south recall the screams still. Dozens of cats, six or seven dogs, fifty calves were lost in my lifetime alone. If you were godless once, you would become pious by necessity, not to any heavenly god but to the earth. So, that summer as our mother boxed up our favorite stuffed animals and our best pots and pans and our few remaining family heirlooms—a Korean doll her mother had given her before death, a bent gold ring adorned with a five-karat diamond, the most expensive thing her mother would ever own—I began to grieve. A loss of home, a loss of distinction, a loss of God.

Chung wailed as our mother made him load boxes into the van. "No," he cried, echoing nearby coyotes, "No, I don't want to go."

I knew better than to argue. I helped our mother with a cumbrous box of dishes, silverware, and though my arms shook and sweat pooled below my eyes in ninety-five-degree heat, I didn't say anything as she paused to scold Chung. "If you'd rather stay, then stay here by yourself. Your daddy will be back in five weeks. I'm sure you'll survive until then."

Our father was in Atchison in a six-week rehab program. Alcoholism. Our mother didn't even wait a week before she started packing.

After Chung shoved the boxes into the backseat, I made him help me with the mattress. We could only fit one, so we chose mine. It was a full bed, more than enough for Chung and I to share. He, nine, was framed like a limp Pinocchio, strings holding him together. I was thirteen, and though my mother preferred to call me "stalky," I was the shortest and lightest in my class.

Because Chung and I were lighter than featherweights, it took time to haul the full-sized mattress from my bedroom at the back of the hallway through the crooked foot-space of the living room where our TV and Nintendo 64 would stay, past the dining room with our great-grandmother's dining table and chairs, the kitchen that our mother had all but emptied. Twice, Chung needed to stop, set the mattress down. All the time, I could hear our mother from the front porch, cooing to the cats we were about to abandon. All the time, my biceps trembled, and my elbow joints began to lock. "Let's go," I kept saying to him, even though I could see he was about to cry, crying, trying not to wail.

Just before we came to the front door, Chung's lips stretched, contorted, and his eyes became hidden by thick lids, a well of tears warning of a flash flood.

"Come on, it's okay," I told him. "We're almost there. It'll be alright."

"I don't want to go."

We got to the front porch, down the four steps, and then he lost it. He didn't drop the mattress, but he stopped in his steps, adolescent cats, limber, snaking between his legs.

"No," he wailed again, and this time he couldn't stop.

Our mother, bent to pet one of the older mother cats, directed her gaze in our direction.

"Jordan, what is taking so long? We need to go."

I tried to get his attention, to lock eyes, but Chung was gone. Irretrievable behind a wave of tears. I could feel my arms going numb, joints flaming, the rib-dented bellies of cats pressing against my calves, the July summer unforgiving, the land unforgiving, cold, already shuttering itself away from me.

And just like that, I became soft. Not a country girl, not a *farm girl*. I watched the mattress descend onto the grass, onto the cat-shit-spotted yard, a flurry of paws and peaked tails rushing for safety. Chung had already given up on the mattress, given up on the farm, so it fell quick, hard. Grass-stained, shit-spotted.

Our mother, she couldn't say a thing, only grin from her place among the cats.

She had found a two-bedroom loft apartment in Salina that had a pool and a laundry room and a decent landlord. These were luxuries that I didn't appreciate at the time. Chung and I had never lived anywhere but the farm. We didn't know what to expect.

For a third time that day, Chung and I carried a mattress. This time up the short flight of stairs leading to our apartment, and up the double-long stairs to the loft, what would become Chung's "bedroom." Because my full-sized mattress had been ruined, we had taken Chung's twin bed, which he would sleep on alone, no box spring, no frame, laid across flattened carpet that smelled like our old milk barn after a decade of abandonment.

After we deposited the mattress, Chung and I paused, secret, in the apartment and cooled down. We took turns fanning the refrigerator door for each other. A moment of peace.

Outside, we found our mother talking to who we assumed to be our neighbor. A mountain lion of a man with a face like it had been stung by a dozen bees and the swelling never went down. He was black-eyed, thin-lipped, beautifully blonde.

"Kent," our mother said in a voice so rarely used we forgot she was our mother for a moment. Only a moment. "This is Jordan, Chung. We just moved from the country," and she said this last word like a curse. The country, where bumpkins, unlike us, unlike her, lived. Even without knowing him, I knew he had never lived in the country. He was a city boy who had moved to this town to be recognized, seen as a treasure.

Kent said nothing to me and Chung. He nodded, yes, but did not speak to us. He and our mother discussed employment opportunities in town, which were apparently numerous for a bright young woman like our mother.

Chung and I celebrated the deposit of the final boxes into the apartment by rubbing ice cubes over each other's faces and arms. Chung, so frail at that time, writhed gleeful with each swipe of the cubes. He had forgotten his tears, forgotten the farm already, and a part of me was relieved, a part of me envious.

That night, our mother slept on a pile of clothes. I slept on another twin mattress that Kent hauled over when he learned of our sparseness. My bedroom, which was an 8′ by 8′ square blocked off by a sliding screen, was dense with heat and what I later identified as the musk of mildew. I couldn't sleep. I thought of the cats, their loneliness, and that alone should've made me cry. They were my best friends, sometimes my only friends. I had helped birth them, had wandered through the farm to locate them when their mothers hid them away—in a maze of hay bales, in just-open tractor cabins, on the smooth, cool tops of garage doors that were never moved from their horizontal position. I couldn't cry. I began to forget my father's face, the smell of alfalfa that clung to your nostrils and didn't let go. I thought of our uncle, who had died so young on that farm, run over by a tractor when he was five years old. His ghost so lonely.

And still, I could not cry.

Because my mother found me short-tempered, she tried to pawn me off on my classmates' parents for a night or two a week.

It wasn't that I was unfriendly to my classmates, that I didn't like any of them or want to talk to them. I just never did outside of school. On the farm, you could grow old among the prairie, the cattle, the glory of searching for intact antlers, bleached cow bones that often appeared in too neat a fashion, too clean.

My point is, you don't need friends in the country. You need reinforcements, for when the land rises up to reclaim you. You need worthy fighters.

During our second week at the apartment, my mother called Molly Rohr's mother and convinced her to have me over for a night. I knew not to protest. I liked Molly. I didn't like her brother. I liked their little town, too, just below four hundred people. One gas station, one grocery store (if you could call it that), and three churches.

Gypsum, Kansas was one of a few smaller towns in Saline County that paled against Salina's literal glow. Fifty-thousand people meant Salina wasn't a town to us. It was a city. Gypsum, being small, being poor, being on the outskirts of the county and in pure rural land, was also the meth capital of central Kansas. Forty labs, many of which were busted before I was thirteen.

Molly, Matt, and their parents lived in a two-story house off of Main Street, the only paved road in town. Their driveway was gravel, a delight to me, as I had begun to choke on the fumes of asphalt, the claustrophobia of narrow city streets. As my mother pulled up in the van and onto the gravel, I felt my disposition better. Yes, Matt was a dick. A creepy dick. But being here, being tangential to the country, was worth it.

Molly's mother, a walking, talking Mama Bear Berenstain turned human, wrapped her arms around me as I shuffled toward their front door, desperate for air conditioning. Our mother never ran the air conditioning in the van. It was a waste of gas. Mrs. Rohr took me in the first hug I had had in months. Maybe a year. I should have appreciated it more, recharged, but I was desperate to be cool, to be indoors.

Inside, I found Matt sitting legs splayed, gym shorts hiked up, Mountain Dew in hand, at the foot of the stairs leading up to Molly's bedroom. He saw me before I saw him. He was grinning, holding his pop can out to me. He was fifteen at the time, about to go into high school because he had been held back in first grade.

"Have a sip?" he asked.

"No thanks."

As I approached the stairs, backpack in hand, he didn't move. He kept grinning, kept his hand outstretched. "Have a sip," he said again.

"No thanks."

I moved to climb the stairs, knee knocking into his, but he scooted to block me. "Come on. You've gotta be thirsty. It's balls-hot out there."

Seeing no course forward, I took the can from him, careful to avoid his hands, which I knew from experience would be sticky, sweaty, and took the smallest sip of Mountain Dew. It was down my throat before I realized it was off. It burned me.

I choked and choked and he laughed.

"Mountain Man Screw."

"What?" I asked, wishing the taste out of my mouth.

"I call it Mountain Man Screw. Mountain Dew, Orange Juice, whiskey."

"That's disgusting," I said, and I pushed past him as hard as I could. He didn't move out of my way, so my knee rammed his shoulder as I passed.

I found Molly leaning against her window, staring out into the street, her shorts riding up and her bra straps fallen over her shoulders. Her tank top had been ripped and tied into a dozen knots. When she saw me, she beckoned me over, pointing toward the window.

"John Wesley is mowing the lawn! Come look."

And she was right. There was John Wesley, a class ahead of us, shirtless and pushing a mower that was surely coated in his sweat. You could have called him handsome, but I chose not to. He was of the breed that bored me. The kind that would delight in wearing a cowboy hat, snake-skin boots. That listened to country music and in the silence of his room sang to the sappy love ballads, the sorrowful laments. He was the type to never leave here, small-town Kansas, but never live in the country, either.

"He is," I said. I asked her how her summer had been, but she didn't answer. Instead, she took my hand and led me out of the room, down the stairs as her brother moved out of the way, and out into the terrible heat once again.

"Hey! Hey, Pretty Boy!" Molly took us across the street without looking both ways. She had to scream, because the lawn mower roared and sputtered. It took her three tries before John noticed Molly hand-to-hip on his freshly-trimmed lawn, me curling into myself, uncomfortable, hot, wishing to be indoors. He didn't grin. He was a half-a-foot taller than me, just above Molly's height. He slammed the mower off. He came up to us and I thought Molly was going to punch him, because I had never seen her stand so erect.

"Hey, you are going to meet Jordan and me right here. Tonight. 9 p.m."

His face didn't change, he just looked down at us, wiping his hands on his shirt.

"I'm doing what?" John asked.

"You heard me. 9. Don't be late."

Inside the house, she laughed like she had to get all the air out of her lungs at once. She dug her hands into her thighs, bent as if to wretch, and laughed, laughed, laughed. This is what I liked about Molly. She saw what she wanted, and she acted on it. She had little capacity to lie, to deceive. I convinced myself I could be like her with enough practice.

Mrs. Rohr prepared us fried chicken and potatoes, sweet corn. It was delicious. She gifted each of us children a chilled glass of strawberry milk after our meal. "We are so happy to have you," she told me, as I rinsed my plate in the kitchen. Another day and I may have hated her for her warmth, for the hidden condescension I would detect in this gesture. Instead, I thanked her.

"I need more good little girls like you around," she said.

"Molly needs a friend like you."

I thanked her again. On my way to rejoin the rest of the Rohrs, I shoved a silly smile from my face. Be cool, Jordan, I told myself. If I wanted Molly to like me, really like me, I needed to be cool.

John met us at exactly nine. He was in a well-fitted white T-shirt, no stains, washed jeans that were tighter than boot cut. This cleanliness surprised me.

He let Molly lead him away from the trim lawn, onto one of the gravel roads leading away from the main artery of Gypsum. We were two houses away from the Rohr's when I heard heavy breathing, footsteps coming from behind. We looked back to see Matt, still in his gym shorts, carrying two Mountain Dews that sloshed over his knuckles as he approached.

"Go away," Molly said flat-toned.

"Jordan invited me," he said, and before I could reply that I hadn't, he was by my side, trying to offer me another Mountain Man Screw. I could smell the alcohol this time. I felt like vomiting.

Molly told him again and again, "go home," but he never did.

Molly led us to the most predictable place for trackless teens to go late at night. The old K-12 school, all brick, windows half-smashed, weeds sprouting through the long-cracked flooring. They had already built a new school out in the country when this one was hit by an F-4 tornado that desiccated half the town twenty years back. Molly guided us through a moonlit hallway, up through the only intact stairwell to a roofless classroom with overturned tables and sun-bleached graffiti.

Molly and John moved themselves to the least exposed corner of the room after only a minute of disinterested conversation with Matt and I. You could say I shouldn't have been surprised. You could say I should have felt betrayed, abandoned.

I did.

No matter what spot I landed in—sitting on the overturned teacher's desk warped by wind and rain, gazing out a glassless window onto nearby fields ripe with gold-red wheat, at a line of trees that passed a song along the wind just for me—Matt followed me. He pressed the cool pop can to my arm. Again and again. Again, I ignored him, moved to another spot. When I settled on the edge of the flooring, letting my feet dangle above the wreckage below, Matt squatted. He didn't sit next to me. *He squatted.* His stupid gym shorts riding up to bear sunless thighs, thighs that wouldn't know a fond touch for a decade at least. When he prodded me with his Mountain Man Screw one last time, I took it from him.

I stared him dead in the eyes, held it out from me.

"Why do you think I would want this?"

Matt, whose mouth had formed a Cheshire-Cat-curve, craggy, began to shrink.

"You know where my Dad is?"

I knew that he did. I had heard Mrs. Rohr quietly reminding him not to bring it up.

Matt became still. He sat his ass down like a proper human being.

"You know and you prod me with this all day long," I said. He opened his mouth to respond, but I cut him off. I wanted to slice his tongue with my interruption. I saw what I wanted. I knew to act on it. "Do you know why you've been pestering me all day long with this, Matthew? Because I do. Do you know?"

Molly was coming over to us, adjusting her bra strap, John following slow behind, eyes glinting white in the moonlight.

"You think it's funny?" I asked. "You're going to end up just like him. A waste of breath."

I threw the pop can. Its neon-green tin reflected the moon. Milky liquid spread in an arc before itself, wetting the litter-strewn flooring. I didn't hear it hit the ground. The gush of blood in my ears was too strong to hear anything else.

When I finally looked away from the ground below, I found myself alone.

John, Molly, and Matt were at the entrance to the school when I found them. We walked back to the Rohr home in silence.

Two days later, Chung, my mother, and I visited our father at rehab. He had hit the halfway mark in the program. He was set to be released on time.

Valley Hope of Atchison contained several modest brick homes, a sprawling cream-painted building with a shaded patio in back. Trimmed lawns. Manicured bushes. Behind the complex, an unruly span of woods.

Our mother was insistent that we all go, and that we all keep secret what we knew would devastate him, what would make these six weeks' progress useless. We didn't tell him we had vacated the farm. She didn't tell him she was separating from him. I could see in her lips, in the flash of a smile, that she wanted to tell him, that she wanted to tell him about Kent, with whom nothing had happened or would happen. But our mother didn't know that yet. But after that flash of a smile faded, I also knew that this feeling, this need to sting, would soon bounce to a need to love and be loved. To mend their broken marriage, even though she would never move back in with him. She couldn't stay hot-blooded for long.

For the second time in two weeks, I was hugged. My father clutched to my rib cage. After a moment, he picked me up and twirled me around. A few tears wet my hair.

"Jordan, you're so tall!" He flattened my hair and patted my shoulders. I couldn't have grown more than a half-inch in the last year. He was buttering me up.

"Chung," our father said, picking him up. "Look at this," and he made Chung flex his arm. "Strong man."

When he set Chung down, he asked more to our mother than Chung, how baseball was going? This was the first summer he didn't assistant coach Chung's baseball team.

Chung just squinted up at our mother. Our mother didn't look at our father, but down at Chung's questioning face. "No sports this summer," she said.

Our father had begun to gain weight, healthy padding around his ribs, his cheeks. For months before he went to rehab, he had been thinning out. His frame, his hair, his skin. The catalyst, the thing that had forced our mother to call our grandparents, was the four-inch chemical burn that had ruptured our father's skin, leading from his elbow toward his thumb. Our mother was convinced he was making meth, and likely doing it, too.

We never did find out the truth. He always denied it.

But before that, he had spent most of his days drunk. Four months before his rehabilitation, we had all gone to Wilson Lake for a family vacation. A recuperation, negotiation. A trip that had ended with Chung and I in the middle of the lake, near-drowning, with our father throwing a fire-touched rock into our mother's face, her skin that scarred, and our father running to a cliff and, in a drunken stupor, flinging himself off the edge into the lake below.

That rehab had not come earlier was more a symptom of pride than anything. Our grandparents had refused the possibility until the burn ripped his skin open. Until it was possible he was manufacturing, until it was possible he would blow the whole farm up. But again, we never knew for sure.

Our mother, father, Chung, and I had lunch together on the rehabilitation center patio. We had come late, arrived just past two, so our lunch was private. He asked us about summer vacation. Had we done anything fun? We didn't know how to answer this. He asked us if we'd found any new kittens on the farm. We said we hadn't. When our mother went to the restroom, he asked us, Are you happy to see me? Have you missed me?

We didn't know how to answer.

The afternoon finished without incident, but as we were leaving, our father pulled me aside, a fresh panic on his face.

"Will you call me next week?"

Chung and our mother didn't notice this. They were headed

to the van.

"Please. Will you call me? I, I just—," and he couldn't finish. I could see tears edging their way to the corner of his eyes. "It's so quiet here."

When he let go of my arm, I said I would. I would call him. How about Thursday? Thursday was great. Anytime.

When my mother, Chung, and I returned to the apartment that evening—it was a three-hour drive back to Salina—we found two notes on our door. One was from Kent, written in elegant handwriting on notebook paper. He said he had a couch for us. A friend was moving and didn't need it anymore. And would we all like to get dinner at Gutierrez this weekend?

The other note, from our landlord: our rent was five days past due. We needed to call him as soon as possible or pay rent and the late fee.

Our mother balled the second notice and placed the first on our fridge.

Dinner with Kent was long. Uncomfortable. It became clear that our mother's idea of this affair and Kent's were incongruent. As our mother referred to this fresh, new start to her life, Kent talked about skyrocketing rent in Salina. About jobs our mother might be interested in, which she took note of without responding. Kent ordered dessert for all of us at the end of the meal, fried ice cream for Chung and me. Double chocolate cake for himself and our mother. When our mother suggested sharing one between the two of them, he laughed.

Our mother didn't laugh. She got the joke, finally. She was the joke. He the simple altruist. Her the self-interested fool.

For days after the dinner, she was more brittle than usual. She screamed at Chung for not eating his Mac 'n' Cheese, to which Chung silently retreated to his loft. There was nowhere to escape her in the apartment, unlike the half-a-dozen sheds and square mile of prairie around the farm. We had little choice but to give in to her. To keep our curses to ourselves.

The next time I was dropped off at the Rohr's house, Matt was nowhere to be seen. Molly hardly said a word to me before or during dinner, which Mrs. Rohr passed off as her teenager turned sulky and disobedient. I didn't want to correct her.

After dinner, I asked Molly what we should do tonight. See what Johnny was doing or go on a walk?

"I don't care. Do whatever you want."

She didn't look up from her dirt-crusted toenails as she painted them glittering green.

I didn't know what to say for a while. I lay on her bedroom floor, sweating, staring out the window.

"What I want is to apologize," I made myself say. "I was mean to your brother."

"I don't care about that," she said, finally making eye contact. "He's a shithead." She went back to painting her nails. When she brushed a knuckle into a wet nail, she cursed and rubbed at the mistake with remover so potent my eyes watered. "But you should be less mean to boys who like you. Otherwise, you'll always be alone."

I didn't respond. When she finally finished both feet, she looked to me again.

"What bothers me is, who talks about their Dad that way? It's," and she blew on her toes. "It's heartless."

I didn't say anything, because there was nothing I could say.

We spent the rest of the night like this. Divorced from each other, from the expectation of friendship. I had shown her a part of myself she disliked and she had shown a part of herself I envied. Ignorance. Innocence.

I called my father on the day we had agreed upon. I told my mother I was going on a walk, and I stole her flip phone from her purse on my way out. A levee stretched miles-long by the

Smoky Hill River—the closest escape to something country-like in town—a shuddering line of trees framing the river, three-acre crops of wheat, alfalfa, lay stunted between the man-made levee and the river. Crops that had little chance to survive, because the land had been deprived its right.

I dialed him while on the levee, but the wind proved too fierce to talk on the phone. Near a youth baseball park, the occasional TINK of a baseball against metal cutting through the wind, I strayed. I approached the river, a ten-foot opening in the trees that extended down to the bank. Heavy rains made the water, iron-red, coil and churn violent against the fine silt. I kept my distance. I'd had enough of near-drowning for a while.

When I settled down, I called him back.

His voice was peaked, flammable.

As we talked about the people he had made friends with, about the coming school year, about the harvest season he was missing (and would never work again; he would go on to construction work because farming was ruinous), I dug my fingers into the soft dirt. I watched the glory of the trees bowing toward the river, pious, and the occasional beaver coast by. I closed my eyes. Imagined a small hut just into the trees. A dainty fire pit that would light up the flowing waters on chilly nights.

"I don't think I can do this anymore."

He had to say it twice, because I hadn't heard the first time. "I can't do this anymore. I want to go home. I want to play *Majora's Mask* with you and play Goku and Gohan with Chung. I don't want to be here anymore."

His voice was frantic, quickening. I knew he was crying. I didn't know what to say. He was waiting, waiting for me to say something, his breaths uneven.

I knew then that I couldn't do it. I couldn't be another person to lie to him. To placate him before the terror would come. All my life, they lied to him. Months before he would die, ten years ahead from now, his parents would say there was no Easter dinner. They would lie and they would never see him living again.

"We moved out of the farmhouse. We have an apartment in town."

I can only tell you that during that phone call, I realized something I was stupid to miss before. I had been denying it. I had believed we all would come back to the farm, or Chung and I would come back to the farm. We would come back to where we had been before. Before our father scarred our mother's face and jumped off a cliff into fetid, unforgiving waters. Before Chung and I almost drowned in those waters. I should have known it all along, but sometimes you have to lie to yourself. Our father was never going to make his way back and neither would we.

"I think you should stay," I told him when I didn't hear a response.

My instinct became again to lie. I fought it down.

"It will be better if you stay. Complete the program. I'll convince her to let us visit you again."

"Dad?"

Still, I heard nothing on the other side. Static. Voices in the background, just outside of comprehension.

Eventually, I ended the call.

Our mother figured out within an hour of my return that I had told him. She didn't have to ask me. She didn't have to acknowledge the misplaced phone or my tear-streaked cheeks. She knew.

That afternoon I hid in my bedroom, holding onto the edge of the screen with all that I could. Her voice became the wind, inscrutable but deafening, until we broke the screen bordering my room—it was never repaired—and she took my hands in one of hers and slapped them for the first and only time I remember. I didn't cry, but I said what every teenager says. Hateful things. Reasonable and unreasonable things. I try to remember Chung not being home, but he was there, as always. He was in his loft, secretly weeping, secretly whispering hateful things, but to who? To her or to me? I don't know. I don't know.

Our father did end up staying the whole six weeks, but no amount of time was going to get him where he needed to be. Within a year, he, too, left the farm. Moved to a one-bedroom house on the other side of Saline County. He became a construction worker. Eventually, our grandparents would reclaim the farmhouse, sheds, silos, but they would never know the land again.

Because Molly never told her mother that she had come to dislike me, that our friendship was kaput, they had me over to their house for a third time in a month. A suffocating number for better friends. Again, we passed pre-dinner and after-dinner in near silence. Matt rarely made eye contact with me. When he did, acid built its way up my throat. A flurry of discomfort and guilt.

When night came, I tried to convince Molly to go to bed early, cut our time together short. She had other plans. Shortly after eleven, when both her parents were long to bed, she slinked out of the house, across the street, initiating a tryst.

I had prepared for a tryst of my own.

When she was gone from the house and out of sight, I too rose from my bed. I grabbed my backpack (full with clothes, water, granola bars, a few utensils, a pocket knife) and tip-toed down the stairs. I found Matt sitting at the bottom of the stairs once again. Mountain Dew in hand, once again. It's like he knew.

"You sneaking out, too?" he whispered.

I continued down the stairs but was blocked from passing.

"Move," I said. He laughed and laughed, louder. I listened for movement in Mr. and Mrs. Rohr's bedroom. "Move," I repeated. "I mean it."

"Aren't you wasting your breath on me?"

I tried pushing past him, but he shoved his shoulder back. "You owe me an apology."

"Do I?" I asked, growing hot. Flammable.

He let me pass by, but as I did, his hand snaked around my wrist.

"Take me with you."

"No."

"Take me with you."

"No."

And then, his wrist pulled me upward. He was trying to drag me back up the stairs. To Molly's room, to his room, I didn't know. I yanked my arm, but he was two years older, stronger. He was just to the top of the stairs when I finally overpowered him. A swift shoulder in the stomach, a whip of my arm.

We both came crashing down the stairs, thunderous.

My hip burned and my leg was pins-and-needles, but I managed to stand, grab my backpack, and hobble to the door. I did look back, as I opened the door. I saw Matt, still on the wood flooring.

I knew the sound would have woken the Rohrs, so I made my best effort to jog down Main Street. To ignore the pain shooting up my leg and back. When I reached the town limits, I slowed pace. Allowed myself to walk, to become reacquainted with the scents and murmurs of the country in its midnight reunion. Whirring locusts, hooting owls, grass folding under gusts of wind, crunching under the paws of soft-footed coyotes.

I didn't know exactly where I was headed, I admit. I must have walked for an hour, the moon providing just enough guidance to see shapes on the edge of the world: tree lines, low-rolling hills, a house, distant, brush-shrouded, abandoned.

Before I came upon the house, half-a-mile from any road, indistinguishable, I knew this would be the place. The earth provided little resistance as I approached. The wind lessened. The world showed itself to me like it hadn't done for weeks.

The house was from pioneer times, constructed of limestone, windows shorn of glass, the door long-rotted away. Only now did

I shine my flashlight, now that I was safe. I saw some possessions, an old shoe, dusty glass jars of emerald and ruby, a half-full bag of what was once potatoes, scattered among the small rooms. A bed frame caving into the ground.

It wasn't perfect, but it would do.

When dawn was near come, I stepped outside the front door. The pocket knife, our father's once—I grabbed it from my backpack and slit a thin line on my palm. Not too deep. I only had a few tubes of Neosporin.

When the sun flayed the horizon, I pressed my palm to the dirt beneath the door. I said a prayer. I made a promise. When the time was right, I would bring little brother, Chung. We would live out our days here, free, content.

I sanitized the cut, wrapped my hand in soft cotton.

I looked on into the coming day.

Two beams of light cut past the sun. Cast the world black in their wake.

S. Shaw

EVERYTHING IS THE CROOKED MAN

(in memory of *Jamar Clark,* killed by the police 11/15/2015)

Everything is a gun
My name is a gun
My laff
A gun
My crooked and rocky path
Behind me a gun too
Large for one man to carry
My turned back
A gun, my
Prone yet unresisting body a
Gun raised
My tongue clicked for release and rebuttal
A gun raised and cocked
My joy
A gun
Raised and cocked and firing.

Everything
Ends here—cold pavement
Taste of trouble on
My lips. I am
Trouble, have been
Trouble
Yet trouble is not
A gun unless it looks
Like me.

RUNNING BLACK HOME

(in memory of *Stephon Clark,* shot and killed by police 3/18/2018)

Stand Black
Black and Forth
Black Up
Look Black
Push Black
Black Out
Hold Black
Draw Black
Throw Black
Black Yard
Shot in the Black
Double Black
Black Talk
Send Black
Black Off
Get Black
Take Black
Fall Black
Black Down
Roll Black
Black Burner
Shot in the Black
I want my life Black
Red and Black
Black The fuck up

I want my time Black
Take me Black
Caress my Black
Black Again
Shot in the Black
Black In the day
Shot in the Black
Black Ground
Shot in the Black
Black To zero
Shot in the Black
It all comes Black around
Black Fence
Black Door
Black Door
Jump Black
Shot in the Black
Black The way you came
Running Black
Black Field in motion
Black Again
Waiting for the time to go Black
I am   Black
I am   Black
I am   Black

The crab is still silent. It doesn't have a head to nod.

Mark Budman

HERE COMES THE SUN: A REMASTERED DIVUS STORY

A (Somewhat) Bilingual Story

The interpreter of dreams and afflictions, известный среди своих как переводчик снов и недугов и среди недругов как "that guy," rolls up his shorts high and wades into the shallow water up to his knees. In addition to shorts, he wears a t-shirt, a floppy hat and a bandana. Whatever may be exposed to the sun, is covered by the sunscreen with SPF 50. He doesn't like the UV light too much, ультрафиолетовые лучи сволочи. It causes pain when people get sunburn, and even more so when they suffer the consequences years later.

Planes land and take off from the nearby Logan airport. They fly low and their bodies momentarily block the sun. Seagulls block it, too. Most of the UV gets through, though, ультрафиолетовые лучи настырные.

The sandy bottom of the lagoon is littered with broken shells. Weeds hug the interpreter's legs. The hair-wide fishes dart back and forth. A little crab fingers the interpreter's foot with its claws, checking if the man has started to rot yet, проверея если переводчик еще не сдох. The interpreter pulls the crab out of the water, and it tries to hide within its shell. The tips of its bone-white claws are sticking out. They look like the fingernails of an old Russian-speaking patient he was interpreting for on several occasions. She was getting worse and worse, and she died, screaming for the whole world to hear, during his morning shift. It all started with the sun exposure for her. People have too much skin.

She hated the sun, she said, and its rays. It's killing us, she said, они нас убивают. Is it the face of the heavens? На самом деле? Where are we to hide? Underwater?

Do you consider me a *divus*, a lesser level of divinity than a *deus*? the interpreter asks of the crab now. Someone who can make a conscious decision about your life and death? You probably think that a *deus* is too high for you, right?

The crab doesn't respond. Maybe out of fear, может он боится. Maybe because it considers itself a stoic. Maybe it thinks a mere crab not worthy to talk even to the lower-rank *divus*?

Do you know that there is a similar word in Russian? *Диво дивное?*

The crab is still silent. It doesn't have a head to nod. Без головы, не возможно кивать.

But maybe the reason it doesn't reply is that it's sick and needs a medical interpreter to communicate with the provider? How one interprets for a crustacean that is lucky enough not to have skin that can be damaged by the sun?

The interpreter lets it go. He returns to his towel on the sand. A seagull eats another crab a few yards away. The crab is still alive, wiggling its legs. The interpreter is sure it's not the same crab. This one is bigger, more mature, and more reserved. The seagull casts an evil eye at the interpreter, the eye of a *divus*, and then returns to pecking.

Переводчик lies down on his towel and dreams about a life in the parallel universe where he knows the language of everyone and everything without being a *divus*, and where the sun is less deadly, and no one is afraid to lift their faces to the heavens.

One day, he'll go there to investigate. Как-нибудь он туда сьездит.

Mary Crow

CAPSIZED

refugees must place faith in boats
even though they know big ones fail
equipped with too few life jackets

days go on carrying precious cargos
of children who can't swim, of small
sisters who vanish, provisional brothers

waves erase every trace of their passage
while the wind keeps re-arranging
sea surface—sharp images disintegrate

in the trough of their rocking, thighs
slip away, hands with no torso, heads
of hair, waves echoing, *Don't care, don't*

not even a final glimpse of tiny nipples
trembling reflex of one hand after another
a photo in the paper shows a vessel tipping

under waves that record their names in
invisible ink in this chilly dissolution who
created countries they prayed to leave

what can the sea now recall of its drowned
in the surf's weary shuffle of flotsam
I don't hear a rollcall of their names

IF YOU LOOK CLOSELY

—Sojourner Truth

Look closely. Come nearer. Peer
into my face, and the lines that
cross and cross it, bind my body,
arms, and between those lines,
can you make out the tiniest
of words stating and restating?
The lines are marks left by invisible
ropes wound round me, so afraid
were those who tied me that they
set their machine to write on me.

What pinpricks did it use? What
sharpest of needles with such
piercing and pain over my eyelids—
DO NOT SEE—over my mouth—DO
NOT SPEAK—I've spent hours
deciphering bits of phrases, "where
darkness" or "not remem" that
their machine worked into me
night and day marring my flesh
and garments till I'm a walking book.

What does my face ask? Can you read
me yet? I'll answer: I'm a not-quite
woman, some claim a not-quite

human. But I'm one who's had
a salty taste of glory, heard a bugle
in the night, and felt dreams explode.
How can I sit idly knowing what
I know? There's rain. Green leaves.
The seasons grieve. Out of
these tattoos, I compose my song.

SPRING FLOOD

The river is undertaking its very own
spring cleaning—ridding itself of clutter
on its banks, flushing trash from currents—
where from we might ask as it throws up
onto land arrowheads and spear points,
a pair of darning shears from the days when
settlers arrived, when natives still hunted
bison, and from later still, keyboard of

a discarded piano, broken candlesticks,
a small wooden cross rubbed smooth over
stones and a porcelain horse head, perhaps
Chinese, then skull of a long-horned
steer, large rounded stones delivered eons
ago by glaciers, tusk of a mammoth, jumble
that hinted at people from 15,000 years ago
who later built Chaco Canyon Pueblo four

stories high, with its 650 rooms, planted
sunflowers, gourds, lived in thatched homes.
The river makes no comment until I
translate its roar or murmur, what it
might tell of the myths of grasslands, Hopi
stories not found in books. But I've got
my history upside down, or at least jumbled—
Is it true you do what you have to do? Or

that what you do is what it is . . . You said,
Look deep into my eyes, is that a haven?
Watch the beveled moon in the center of
each pupil, what wishes are embedded in that
pale moonscape? A tiny rover walks the dust
of craters and endures whirlwinds, clouds
which means water somewhere, maybe a way
out of absolute desert, or butterflies migrating.

I will probably never be a lapsed vegetarian, but surely being a lapsed platypus is something far more pitiful.

Richard Prins

THE LAPSED VEGETARIAN[1]

I know a man in Tanzania who dreams of not eating meat.

We met at a bar in Dar es Salaam. He offered me a joint in exchange for a beer. He even offered to get his friend who grills shish kebab in the street to give me a free meal, so desperate was he to besiege his liver.[2] When I explained that I didn't eat meat, he told me his life story. Sent to college in the States, he dropped out during his first semester to pursue a squatter's life of anarchy

---

1 I wrote this essay eleven years ago for an undergraduate creative writing course on "The Lyric Essay." I wanted to craft it as a scientific research paper getting gnawed open from the inside by a narrative personal essay. But I didn't know how to write a scientific research paper, so I failed to execute the essay's "lyric" element. Later, I lost the essay to a hard drive failure, but kept thinking about it as the years went by, for I had reached inside myself and nearly grasped something essential. During a recent move, I found a copy tucked inside my old Lyric Essay course packet, marked with a classmate's perfunctory line edits. I typed it up—cringing at my own verbosity, my sophomoric fetish for lengthy words with Latin roots. I present it here, having excised only the most grotesque embellishments.

2 When I realized this essay wouldn't qualify as "lyric," I considered coaxing it into the "unreliable narrator" genre, but felt too sincerely about the material to code myself as literary trickster. However, that didn't stop me from lying a heck of a lot in this essay. I didn't consider it dishonest, because I lived by Picasso's credo, "Art is a lie that makes us realize the truth." That meant I could make shit up. I had a loose grip on reality anyhow, on account of my poetic pretensions and liberal dabbling with hallucinogenic drugs. So this essay did, in fact, have an unreliable narrator; I just did nothing to signal my unreliability. And here in the third line is the first outright lie in the essay: My friend (he became my closest friend in Tanzania, not just some scroungy rando I met at a bar) did offer me the joint, but we didn't discuss meat until the second or third time we met. Why did I say we did? It was a shortcut to the topic of the essay—much easier than telling the truth.

and hedonism in the Lower East Side. He initially converted to veganism to impress a girl, but it blossomed into a full-time obsession. He joined Food Not Bombs, cooking meatless meals for the Tompkins Square Park demimonde. After several years, he was deported back to Tanzania, where his mother sheared his dreadlocks and forced him to eat meat again. For no self-respecting African refuses what is cooked for them. They don't have the privilege of Food Not Bombs coming to their local Skid Row every Sunday. *Ukienda kwa wenye chongo, vunja lako jicho!* she scolded him with Swahili proverbs.[3] *When going among one-eyed people, put out your own eye.*

I thought of Oedipus, watching him wince at his beer. In that wince, I saw his plight, his exile, his loss. I knew that every time he masticated a burnt corpse, it drove him further from his East Village stomping grounds. He began rhapsodizing about his plan to return. He will pass through Mexico to foil the INS (he didn't know that INS had become ICE as part of its post-9-11 transplantation to the Department of Homeland Security).[4] He will parade down St. Mark's Place with a *DIE YUPPIE SCUM* placard. He will stiff NYU students with fake bud in Washington Square Park.[5] He will mix it up once more in the mosh pit at CBGB's (I

---

3 I have no reason to believe his mother ever said this. It just happened to be one of my favorite Swahili proverbs, and I wanted to show off my fluent Swahili after spending the prior semester abroad at the University of Dar es Salaam.

4 Neither did I. I made the correction when retyping the essay. While I had always considered DHS a crypto-fascist entity, my concerns (like not getting wiretapped by my own government) now seem quaint. I lacked the capacity to imagine the atrocities our bureaucrats would visit upon immigrants, asylum-seekers, and their young children.

5 This isn't a lie that makes us realize the truth; it's a lie in service of my desire to suppress the truth. My friend certainly hustled and stole and broke a lot of laws when he was living in the States as a squatter and eventual crack-cocaine addict. But I wholly fabricated this example of his chicanery. For something similar had happened to me. Two guys stepped out of a McDonald's and complimented my clothes (I wore then, as I wear now, billowy, patterned Senegalese pants and radiant dashikis, and I was ravenously susceptible to compliments). They asked if I smoked weed. (I

didn't have the heart to tell him that vaunted institution was now a designer menswear boutique). Above all, he will dumpster-dive (with so many new artisanal vegan dumpsters to choose from) and never again eat meat.

In this lapsed vegetarian, I saw kaleidoscopic projections of myself. At thirteen I became a longhair, at fourteen a Communist, at fifteen a vegetarian. I loved having one more thing to make incendiary pronouncements about. I loved taunting anybody sighted gnawing on a drumstick with the specter of docile, disemboweled chickens. I especially enjoyed opining that cannibalism was more morally defensible than common carnivorism, since it binds predatory behavior within the mutual purview of a single species. If morality was a marching band, I had found my sousaphone.

In dreams, I eat meat. Usually spaghetti bolognese. A forkful is guided toward my mouth by a hand that isn't attached to anything. As soon as I realize what I am allowing to happen, I spit up the half-chewed beef and vermicular noodles. Is my subconscious alerting me that I need more protein, or warning me of the nightmarish peril of becoming a lapsed vegetarian?

Then there was Scott. Never had I met anyone for whom a vegan diet was such a centerpiece of identity. I met him while

---

didn't, but nobody believed me, so I affected a stoned gaze and said *yeah sure man*). They promised to bring primo shit right to my dorm—I just had to prove I wasn't a cop (by showing the bills in my wallet weren't marked). "Man, I've been arrested!" I defended my honor while extracting all my cash. One of them made a show of inspecting the serial numbers. Then they turned around and walked in opposite directions. I didn't know which one of them had my money. I just knew I wasn't getting it back. What was I going to do about it? Tell the police? Of course not. I opposed their very existence. But the real reason I wouldn't tell the cops (or anybody else, ever, until now) was pure, simple mortification. I, a native New Yorker, had been hoodwinked like some caricature of a tourist. I couldn't write about something so humiliating, not for a classroom full of callow suburbanite Columbia students. Instead I conjured a story of my friend conning a rube like me. (Dear subconscious, give this footnote a footnote: Does that mean I secretly suspected my friend would mug me?)

leaving an antiwar protest with two friends to get some pizza. He was walking towards the demonstration, a latecomer with a pointy goatee and lion's mane of dreadlocks. Each fuzzy blonde lock was festooned with neon beads. Both his wrists were barnacled with dozens of colorfully-beaded bracelets. He asked if he could go wherever we were going. We were teenagers. He was clearly in his thirties. We asked his age. He frowned, scratched at his scalp, and settled on an answer: "I don't believe in saying my age." But he didn't seem creepy so much as dazed. We let him tag along to the pizzeria, where he announced he wasn't going to have pizza, because he was vegan. He asked for a slice of pizza with no cheese. Told that slice didn't exist, he wondered if they couldn't just fry him up some dough. He was offered garlic knots. He shook his head no; he didn't have any money.

But he did have a pin of Dennis Kucinich's[6] smirking face. "He's vegan, so he's the only candidate who truly understands peace."

"I'm for Howard Dean," my friend said.

"Screw that dude! He looks like just the kind of guy who would stuff his face with a hamburger. Like, he opens his mouth to talk and I swear I see a hamburger inside it."

I thought I could impress him by mentioning I was vegetarian.

"Cool. You're halfway there."

My two friends[7] didn't mention they were also vegetarians, because they didn't share my love of hirsute wingnuts. Besides, they were vegetarians with different motives. The Dean supporter gave up meat for "health reasons" (euphemistic for anorexia, a diet

---

[6] Dennis Kucinich was a vegan member of Congress who ran a long-shot campaign for the Democratic presidential nomination in 2004. While Scott did support his candidacy, it was actually me wearing that pin of his elfin face. I must have been ashamed to confess having championed such a kooky, nebbishy vanity project as the Kucinich campaign.

[7] I was with two friends when I met Scott, but they weren't vegetarians. I purposefully conflated them with two other friends in order to discuss the disparate philosophies behind vegetarianism (and make a mean-spirited, latently misogynistic dig about eating disorders).

made far more tenable by arbitrary elimination of most American food products). The other friend also had no moral opposition to the consumption of meat, but found animals filthy and didn't want anything to do with them, certainly didn't want pieces of their flesh in his mouth.

An astute observer might wonder why he wanted anything to do with me. At fifteen I gave up meat, and at sixteen I mostly gave up showering, conserving water for the sake of our ailing planet. At least pigs take exfoliating mud baths on a daily basis. Not so any hippie worth his tie-dyed stripes. Thus it would be hypocritical for me to call animals dirty, but can anyone deny they're gallingly stupid?

No, I've never been much of a PETA poster child. I didn't stop eating animals out of any sense of bonhomie. I especially disdain dogs and the people who own them. Growing up on the Upper West Side of New York City, my elevator rides were plagued with little old ladies who insisted on filtering conversation through their damp-snouted, floor-sniffing pups. *My, Pookie, aren't his pants colorful? Oh dear, Fluffy, aren't we worried it might rain today!* At times like these, I honestly would not have minded if both pooch and madame were sniped by tranquilizer darts and hauled off to the nearest abattoir to be sawed into succulent smithereens. And I would gladly recruit less compunctious friends to feast on their sausaged remains.[8] But I would never partake in such a feast myself, because that would be immoral.

Immoral why? Immoral because I once brimmed with half-baked notions of social justice and recognized those notions had to include other living creatures. So I phased mosquito-swatting out of my life. I staged interventions against cockroach lynch mobs.[9]

8 This was me posing as unreliable narrator. I didn't truly harbor any desire to mutilate old ladies or feed them to my friends. But any reasonable reader could infer as much, so this is actually among the least dishonest sections of the essay.

9 Even the most half-baked notions of social justice wouldn't extend the right of due process to common household pests, and thus wouldn't

And finally, after much deliberation, I informed my mother that I would no longer eat meat.[10]

She was much more understanding than my Tanzanian friend's mother had been. She undertook a midlife crisis, defuncting her consultancy business and ordering tome upon tome of vegetarian cookbooks. Perhaps she'd seen names like Caesar Chavez[11] materializing on my bookshelf and feared I would take up hunger-striking as a hobby if she didn't appease my gustatory whims. My father, in solidarity, attempted a midlife crisis of his own. He dug a viola out of a closet, dusted it off, and taught himself to play again. Surely he imagined that his endless scales, shrill and awry as a theremin, would comfort my mother as she boiled vegetable stock in the kitchen. My brother, on the other hand, confronted for the first time by a flaccid chunk of tofu, announced that he was now a pure carnivore who would never again touch a vegetable, except to remove the pickle or lettuce leaf wedged between burger and bun. This confirmed my mother's suspicions that his preppiness was a strategy of rebellion against my hippie persona. But she always made sure our dinner table was rationed with herbivorous and carnivorous options, my brother and I seated on opposite ends of the family see-saw.[12]

Scott resurfaced in my life every so often to join me at a

---

equate a mere cockroach-stomp with the extrajudicial murder of thousands of black Americans.

10 False. I told all my friends I would stop eating meat in the new year, but didn't bother informing my mother (the woman who cooked most of my meals) of this decision. She found out on New Year's Eve, when a friend teased me, "Your last chance to eat meat and all you got is Chinese takeout?" Seeing how confused my mother was, he burst out laughing, "You didn't know Richie was going veggie, did you?"

11 I never owned a book by Cesar Chavez, so file this fib under "performative wokeness." However, I did undertake multiple hunger strikes the year before I became a vegetarian, protesting flagrant abuses of parental authority, like when they wouldn't let me date a heroin addict.

12 I should note that this paragraph, while accurate in spirit, commits too many generalizations and hyperboles to enumerate.

demonstration or just gallivant about the city. I enjoyed having my own personal[13] burnout Bodhisattva, who flitted from protest to rave to Phish show, accumulating beads and psychedelic drugs by the handful. He supported his lifestyle by canvassing door-to-door for an imaginary non-profit called Millennium Democracy, armed with a manifesto of run-on sentences proclaiming lofty goals like "End World Hunger!" As far as I could tell, his monetary collections only ever ended his own hunger. Once I asked Scott about the ethics of his operation. He replied, without any detectable sense of irony, "Have you ever heard the saying 'think globally, act locally?'" Nothing's more local than your own belly; the man really believed he was saving the world by spanging for grub, as long as the grub was vegan.

Scott occasionally disappeared for months to try his luck on the West Coast, but always returned when the bad vibes became too plentiful, or when he encountered too many people who claimed vegetarianism, only to be seen eating fish. "The pescetarian," he complained upon one of his returns, "Is the only true enemy of the people."[14]This was in Union Square, where he had called me from a payphone[15] wondering if I would come guide him through his homecoming acid trip.

The man was hungry, but he had no money. His hyperblasted serotonin receptors convinced him that he must go to Korea Town, where somebody would gift him with a bowl of hot and

[13] Creepy word choice, no? Almost like I thought of him as some quirky talisman I purchased at a curio shop.

[14] It's a good line, right? I'll take the credit; Scott never said it, though he often seemed to believe it.

[15] Why did I say he called me from a payphone? The real story is much more interesting. Scott was crashing at my apartment in the Bronx. One of my roommates was a heroin addict who had invited a fellow addict to sleep on our couch rent-free. So I invited my insufferable hippie friend to crash on the floor. Was this an act of charity or passive-aggression? Probably both. Scott showed up with a bottle of tequila and a strip of acid as house gifts, but quickly wore out his welcome.

sour soup.[16] "The vibes," he explained, "are good tonight." But it was after midnight. Most eateries were closed. After hours spent searching for this elusive soup, he finally deigned to dumpster-dive. But he didn't even get as far as a proper dumpster. On the corner, he spotted an open takeout container in a garbage can. A half-eaten chicken parmesan. Teeth marks serrating the soggy lukewarm meat, its fried crust absorbing red sauce. Scott seized it, and took a huge famished bite.[17]

"Scott! That's chicken!" I yelped, too late to save him from defiling his mouth.

He whipped around, locking panicked eyes with mine. Between us, nothing but his terror. Still he tried to shrug it off. "So what, dude? It's free. I had nothing to do with it dying, so you know, I can eat it. I'm a freegan. If it's free, it's vegan."

I'm not a Communist anymore. I more or less stopped attending protests after the crowning achievement of getting myself arrested at the 2004 Republican Convention.[18] But it's okay to be a lapsed Marxist. Most intelligent people are. Even the Neocon nutcases who bequeathed us our current kakistrocracy[19] were disgruntled Trotskyist scholars, eager to manifest a warped

---

16 My roommate and another friend were also tripping on Scott's acid; it was actually the other friend who became fixated on hot and sour soup. Did I erase him from the essay for compression's sake? Or because I had recently had sex with him and hadn't told my girlfriend about it? Unreliable narrators can make unreliable lovers, too.

17 This section commits the most malicious lie in the entire essay. Scott never bit into any animal product. This was libel, pure and simple. I was writing an essay about lapsed vegetarians, so I needed my uber-vegan to lapse. I'm sorry, Scott, wherever you are, for impugning your integrity.

18 Ever since Trump was elected president, I have been getting myself arrested as often as I can manage it—eight times and counting. At its heart, this essay was about the lapsing of my political and moral convictions. But now I have a fascist in the White House and a four-year-old daughter to worry about. I find myself regaining some sense of purpose. Maybe that will include treating my friends—and the truth—with more respect.

19 A decade later, we're ruled by a completely different cast of kakistocrats, conveniently allowing those Neocons to rehabilitate their images.

Permanent Revolution, whether in Southeast Asia or in the Middle East. So say what you will about the moral compass of lapsed Marxists; at least they aren't lacking for motivation.

But a lapsed vegetarian? There is no way to spin such ignominy. Vegetarianism is determined negatively, by what you don't do: eat meat. But if you were to drop dead tomorrow, you wouldn't eat meat anyway. So merely being vegetarian has no more positive impact on the world than being a corpse. And if you can't muster such a moribund substitute for resistance, then what is left of you?

That's why I stare at my fingers in terror whenever they pluck a wafting mosquito out of the air and carelessly squash it. When the exterminator makes his monthly visit to spray my apartment, I don't chain myself to the radiator or chant radical slogans. But afterwards my spine creaks with guilt for failing to intervene against the slaughter.

If I don't watch out, I could become just like them.

Whenever someone mentions they used to be vegetarian, I listen closely. What caused them to give it up? When did that bedrock of diet and identity begin to feel like a weighty, ostentatious necklace they no longer wished to wear?

Several rationales are common. They became anemic (so eat some goddamn spinach). They couldn't afford it (as if living off pizza is so expensive). They married an animal-eater (show me one prenuptial agreement that stipulates the consumption of sentient beings by all interested parties). Most of the time, they act like it's no big deal. Most of the time, I know better than that. I just think about Scott. Whom I haven't seen since parting ways at the PATH station.[20] He planned to nap on a bench, tingling with humiliation and acid afterglow, until he could catch a morning train back to his charitable sister's basement in Paterson, New Jersey. But I did get a voicemail from him last month. I saved it,

---

20 We actually rode the subway back to the Bronx. But when my roommates kicked him out, he went back to his sister's.

for the sake of posterity, for the sake of my integrity.[21]

"Hey dude, it's Scott! I'm back in Jersey. Trying to get some work, you know, so I applied for a job at the Stop & Shop and put you down as a reference. So uh, if anyone calls asking for Richard Platypus,[22] like, say good things about me."

What began with a guilty bite of chicken ended with Scott selling out to the man.[23] That's why I can't swallow the bolognese sauce, no matter how hungry the dream. It would mean complacence. A one-way ticket into the bowels of corporate America. I don't think Scott got the job. They never called me to check on his reference, probably just assumed he had fleas.[24] I like to think that if he ever had to ring up somebody's purchase of bacon, he'd give them one of his lackadaisical tongue-lashings. But I've lost my faith in him. You can't count on a broken man to resist anything, let alone a predatory world.[25]

---

21 For all the vicious lies I told about Scott, I believe this voicemail was transcribed verbatim.

22 "Richard Platypus" was the name on my Facebook and Myspace accounts, and the name that appeared in the top right corner of this essay when I handed in the assignment; I felt a powerful affinity for the duck-billed taxonomical misfit. I dropped this moniker some time after receiving my first rejection letter from a literary magazine, which told me, in essence, "If you're trying to be funny with the platypus thing, it's not working." I will probably never be a lapsed vegetarian, but surely being a lapsed platypus is something far more pitiful.

23 My professor pointed out that I was a student at an Ivy League university—not the best vantage point to sling any shit about selling out to the man.

24 An assumption I shared, having acquired a bad case of head lice after Scott and I trekked by bus to Washington D.C. to attend the March For Women's Lives (where Scott, self-proclaimed feminist, made a point of asking every volunteer distributing free prophylactics if they had any XL-sized condoms).

25 The subtext of the essay is that the broken man was me. The subtext of these footnotes is that I lacked the self-awareness to understand the subtext I had written, or to recognize how broken I really was.

Michael Kleber-Diggs

DISPATCH FROM MIDDLE AMERICA

for Murray Middle School, St. Paul, Minnesota

The Karen are here and the Hmong. Ethiopians, Eritreans, and the Somali are here. They are here from Europe, Mexico, and Canada. Americans are here, first generation and seventh generation and indigenous. Black and white, Asian—every race and ethnicity—they are all here. Christians and Jews, Muslims and Hindus, Buddhists and UUs and atheists, so many faiths are here. A single Rastafarian is here. He's white, his colorful clothes always adorned with the leaf of his sacred herb. He walks among girls in abaya and chador, hijab, dupatta. The comically tall and the very short. The wealthy and the poor. Children of the hyper-educated; children of the semi-literate, broken children and blessed children. Here. Gay boys are here. Lesbians and bisexuals, trans and queer kids are here. They are all here. Each of them and all of them. Here with their dreams and desires, their dramas and disturbances. Some flowers blossoming in radiant display, some seeds wanting water and fertile soil. But here. They laugh, and they cry. Some hit each other, some fuck each other. Some try smoking or drinking or pills or love. But they all bounce about here, for your consideration, perpetually in flux at a single middle-school in Saint Paul, in Minnesota, in the Upper-Midwest of America. Half asleep and completely alive with their phones and their ear buds, their affectations and their urgency—all as if to say: look at me. Please don't look at me. Help me. Please leave me alone. Go away please. Never leave me. Here, please. Here.

EVERY MOURNING

Morning: walking my neighborhood, I come upon a colony
of ants busy at work. I take care not to step on any and miss

them all, then encounter up a way, a fellow traveler greeting
the day. I am frightening her. No. She is afraid of me.

Is she an introvert? Is she a neighbor? Is she just in from the 'burbs,
from the country? Is she scared of the inner city? Am I the inner city?

Is she racist? Shouldn't I be the wary one? Or is she a survivor
like me? It can't be what I'm wearing: khakis, blue & white

checkered button-down shirt, and the nylon sandals
I favor because they're comfortable, not fashionable.

My feet can breathe in them.
You guys, I am the nicest man on earth.

And I want to shout *morning*! But just then a weaver or
carpenter, just then a pharaoh or fire or pavement, just

then a little black ant struggles by alone. Alone.
And in that moment, I want us to give ourselves over

to industry, carry the weight of the day together, lighten
it. I want to be a part of a colony where I feel easy

walking around. Cool as the goddamn breeze. Where
I can breathe, build structures sturdier and grander

than this—but the woman crosses to the other side
of the street, and I do what I usually do: retreat into

myself as far as I can, then send out whatever's left.

"Caffeine is not good for the baby."

Mehdi M. Kashani

GOOD GIRL

A flight from Tehran to Toronto, with a four-hour layover in Rome. Parting from a husband to reunite with a sister. An exacting journey for Mina, thirty-five-weeks pregnant. Her husband's visa had been denied, but they both agreed she should go and deliver the baby in Canada, despite her fear of traveling alone, her dread of pregnancy complications. It was the right decision, an act of valor for the baby's future, Mina tells the old lady sitting next to her on the plane.

"Good girl. Good girl," the old woman wheezes through her almost toothless mouth.

She's too old. For the stretch of time they are in the air, she has the same chance of dying as Mina's baby has to be born. Such a horrible thought, Mina scolds herself.

The old woman stares at Mina's belly. "A beautiful girl."

"How do you know it's a girl?" Mina and her husband don't want to know.

"Oh, I can read it from your face, dear." Now, the woman is gazing at Mina's face, as if she is deciphering the baby's gender right then.

Mina smiles at the prospect of having a girl, then shifts in her seat, to her sides, left, right, left and then right again. Not a modicum of sleep until the plane begins its descent. She shuts her eyes as the wheels touch the ground. When she pops them open, she finds the old woman peering at her belly.

On her way to the gate in the vast Leonardo Da Vinci Airport, Mina treats herself to a coffee. A minor dalliance she thinks she's earned, considering the sacrifice she's making for the baby.

She flops into a chair, gazing out at the planes on the tarmac. She FaceTimes her sister, who's moving about with a towel on her head. Halfway into their chat, Melody asks about her seatmate. Any garrulous dudes?

"A sweet old woman," Mina says. "She couldn't take her eyes off my belly."

Her sister laughs. "Be careful! She might be an Aul."

Mina sips her coffee. "A what?"

"Oh, pregnancy brain." Melody sounds disappointed. "Grandpa's book of myths and superstitions? The old crone with the blue dagger who steals babies and leaves the mothers to die." Pause. "Why am I telling you this?" Another snort peppered now with edginess.

Mina sighs, fighting against her drooping eyelids. "Don't worry, she was like a hundred years old. My most immediate enemy is insomnia."

Her sister assures her it won't get better, but a comfy bed awaits her in their house. They exchange virtual kisses and hang up and then Mina raises her cup only to hear someone on her left, "Caffeine is not good for the baby."

It's the old woman. Startled, Mina drops the cup. The woman lunges and saves it in a brisk move. Only a few drops sprinkle on Mina's loose gray dress, but it's enough to make her howl.

"Easy. Easy." The old woman produces a rag and rubs it on Mina's belly. "We don't want her to get hurt."

"What are you doing here?"

"Travelling. Remember?"

The crone drags her feet to toss the coffee cup. From the loudspeakers they announce the boarding, inviting passengers requiring assistance to go first.

"Let's go, we both need assistance."

When Mina learns the old woman is sitting next to her on this flight too, she accepts it with mute passivity. At least she has the aisle seat, easier to escape if it comes to that.

In the air, the woman is eerily quiet. She's too small and frail to be a threat to anyone, pregnant or not. Mina eyes over her loose shirt, at the top of her breasts. Auls have sagging breasts, Mina remembers, so long and sinking they'd throw one over their shoulders, like the tail of a shawl. This one doesn't. Well, auls also have clay noses. Mina snorts, picturing the clownish face.

She leafs through the plane magazine, another attempt at luring her brain to shut down. Then she reclines her seat and closes her eyes, hoping the next time she opens them she'll be in Toronto. The plane hums along, like a lullaby. She likens herself, in that cramped position, to a baby in the womb. She rubs her belly, not sure if she's doing this for real or in a dream. Only a few hours left until she reaches safety. With Canadian citizenship, her child won't have the troubles Mina has had to bear in a country full of hardships. Her child will be free to choose what to study, where to travel, what to wear, which languages to speak. Mina sees her child in a lucid dream, she wills it to change age or gender, but always in the streets of a foreign land, free as a bird. *She's coming.* Something hisses in her ears. *She's coming.* A trembling voice. Mina jolts awake. The lights are out. Absolute silence except for the engines. The old woman's seat is empty. When did she slide past Mina? *She's coming.* The voice originates from the figure occupying Mina's legroom, crouching over her crotch, her veiny hands trying to part Mina's legs. How can she even fit there?

Mina screams.

The lights turn on. People shift in their seats. The old woman raises her head, an index finger held aloft. *Shhh.*

The stewardess arrives to check on Mina. She gasps at what she sees.

"Does anyone know how to deliver a baby?" the stewardess yells.

A hubbub ripples across the plane, people expressing their

wonder, calling for God and Jesus.

"In Canada," Mina croaks. "Not here."

She wriggles out of her seat. The crone's hands clutch at her waist, so firm as if she's an extension of Mina's body. Unable to stand, Mina rolls over and lies on the floor, in the aisle, bringing up her knees.

People huddle around her. The stewardess tries to disperse them. The voice on the loudspeaker invites everyone to stay calm, asks if anyone is a doctor. *Push.* The old woman is pressing Mina's stomach. *Breathe.* Mina looks at the people towering over her.

"Help me," she pleads to the constellation of heads. Raising her upper body, she stretches her arm and stabs at the old woman. It feels like she plucks something from the witch's face. She opens her fist: a slightly transfigured round clay chunk with two holes.

Mina shrieks, "She has a blue dagger." She lifts the palm of her hand as if to prove it.

The passengers click their tongues, shake their heads, make the tiny ceiling lights appear and disappear.

I can see her head. One more push.

"No, no," Mina shouts, banging her head on the hard floor. She hears the baby's wails. *Good girl, good girl.* Mina feels empty inside, unburdened. She raises her head, seeking the old woman. But she only hears that lullaby voice receding, singing over the newborn's cries. *Good girl. Good girl.*

Mina is exhausted now. Unmindful of the surrounding racket, she turns her head to her side and glimpses the mound of clay in her hand, unshaped and soaked in sweat.

MY ULTIMATE THOUGHT IS THIS

In conversation, a friend from my youth
who worked for a time as a prison guard
saw fit to say, *Michael, you don't know much –*
lots of these convicts are just feral beasts.
On hearing his words, I surrendered faith.
I wound myself up so I could pounce down
on his beliefs—pinned him down hard, showed
him my teeth, growled in his face from my
far better view (I despised his and him).
Chewing on the cheek of his claim, the next
to last thought to enter my head was this:
only a beast thinks a man is a beast.

Occasionally, my mother asked me to take food next door.

Rahme Al-Mghayzawi

THE HOUSE NEXT DOOR

Translated from the Arabic by Essam M. Al-Jassim

It was common for my mother to say, "We have new neighbors," after passing the house next door.

The turnover generally occurred in the usual manner—nothing out of the ordinary. New faces moved in, settled down, and eventually moved out. Whispers and footsteps appeared, increased, and then dissipated. My mother and I remained in a constant state of anticipation over the next arrival.

We grew accustomed to the eyes of newcomers looking at our house, examining our comings and goings. Peeking faces would occupy the house for one or two months, but never longer than six. Over time, with the jumble of nameless faces, we lost any sense of intrusion. Our relationship with the neighboring house, and its occupants, was far from a strengthening bond. It was more a matter of getting accustomed to a steady rotation of people.

One morning, I awoke to a persistent knocking on our front door. I had lingered in bed far too long, but still I drew the blanket over my head, loath to rise. But the knocking only grew louder. I lumbered out of my room. The insistent pounding also woke my mother. When I heard her feet shuffling down the hall, I joined her. I was standing a step behind her when she opened the door.

He stood uncomfortably, wringing his hands as if sorry to be intruding. His soft black hair stuck to his scalp with dense sweat. Barely managing to hold back tears, he pleaded, insisted we follow him. He gestured wildly toward his house, each frantic movement painting his fear in the air.

When we entered his house, a woman lay bleeding on the floor, clearly in excruciating pain. The room was bare except for a bed and a small cupboard. Her husband stood at the doorway, exhibiting the same anxiety he had shown on our doorstep.

My mother slowly approached the bleeding woman and helped her into a sitting position. A newborn baby—a boy—lay lifeless next to her, a silent lump of flesh and blood. My mother nodded sympathetically and motioned for the woman's husband to approach. Tension and panic dominated every feature of his face. I had to look away. But at the sound of his whimper, I looked back. He walked slowly with a heavy step to pick up his silent son. Tears filled his eyes.

We spent the next two nights at their house, trying to help the woman.

Every word the man said to my mother in the following days expressed a fierce internal trembling. His wife, to my surprise, showed no emotion after all that had happened. Instead, she seemed absurdly concerned by the foul odor and the dampness that the abundance of unused milk from her breasts caused. She focused on the frequent need to change her bra, remaining silent and stoically calm as if nothing extraordinary had occurred, as if these events were outside the framework of her interest and attention.

My mother and I stopped by to visit the woman for several days afterward. She didn't talk about her family, her husband's family, or where they had come from. Her complaints, which now came frequently, involved her third miscarriage of a son and the copious amounts of wasted milk. As time passed, she gradually discouraged our visits and secluded herself in her house for the last stage of her grief.

Occasionally, my mother asked me to take food next door. One day, while approaching their house, I heard the woman screaming—threatening, cursing, and accusing her husband of peeping at the neighbors' daughters. The altercation was explosive and could be heard through the door. The woman cursed her father, who had forced her to marry him. And he reviled his mother, who had chosen her to be his wife. She wept more for herself than for her stillborn son. As I heard them arguing, I imagined her husband's face expressing the same worry that had been visible the morning he'd knocked on our door.

Having shared in the tapestry of our neighbors' lives, I convinced myself they would not be like those before them who had moved on. However, my mother felt confident the familiar ritual would unfold as usual and our neighbors' faces would change within half a year. My mother knew the village couldn't retain strangers for longer than that. It always spat out new faces, and everyone departed.

Julie Cadwallader Staub

LISTEN

What sound do the vertebrae make
in the back of a neck when they give way?
do they snap and splinter like a wishbone?
do they quietly collapse, crush the windpipe beneath?

What happens to the uniformed knee
when it lifts up, straightens from a body gone limp?
will it haunt its master with the memory of that final shove
when one human life changed from struggle to gone?

We know the sound that vertebrae make
the sound of a throat collapsing
we've heard it again and again:
I can't breathe

and we know what happens to the knee that bends
that pushes until it kills
we've heard it again and again:
nothing.

But what happens if the sound
of vertebrae broken in a Black man's neck
reverberates across a nation
ignites again that deep, long simmering fire

born of centuries of outrage and mourning
for Eric and Michael and Sandra and Ahmaud and

for Emmett and Trayvon and Breonna and Martin and
Malcolm and Medgar and Addie Mae and Cynthia and Carol
and Carole?

Will our nation's backbone
—engineered to uphold white male supremacy—
be broken, dismantled

transformed vertebra by vertebra
to stand
and to stand up
for justice?

SISTERS

Such a love of a dog! the woman exclaims
as she bends to pet Belle at the playground.

She's a rescue, I say, *found*
nearly starved to death with puppies.

I shake my head and wonder aloud
How could anyone abandon such a sweet dog?

She snaps *I'm a foster mom!*
You should see what they do to children!

By the time my dog nudges me from my standstill
I am lost in a labyrinth of thought

Where does anger end and sorrow begin?

Does anger sputter to a halt when sorrow takes its first breath?
Does sorrow dissolve when anger is in the lead?

Or do they travel side by side,
even hand in hand, like sisters?

And how did Kate find her way through the sorrow of losing
her sister?
Did she ever find an end to her rage over losing Maddie to a
dealer

a dealer who waited until Maddie was dopesick, her craving
excruciating,
until Maddie would do anything to make it stop

and then he pounced, knowing
you can sell a bag of dope only once

but a girl?
again and again and again.

With gratitude to Kate O'Neill, who wrote: "Trafficked: How the Opioid Epidemic Drives Sexual Exploitation in Vermont"

Aside from being near their office, this particular sandwich shop had the advantage of offering sweet potato fries, a favorite to both.

V LIKE VEGETABLE

1.

The doctor pointed at a complex map of nerves and then turned to her patient. The patient, Grace Hudson and her husband, Javad Arasteh, stared at the map, bewildered, not knowing what exactly to look for—a cross on a treasure map, an extra knot, or a spare part. The doctor explained with an annoyingly professional calmness:

"You see, this is a type of neurological paralysis that can sometimes affect facial nerves. Do you see the path? Its root cause is not quite clear. It is likely to have been caused by a virus that attacked a nerve. Or it might be due to a limited autoimmune disease. But overall, it does not appear to be a progressive problem. It is not dangerous either. Unfortunately, there are things you might no longer be able to do, as I am sure you have already noticed yourself. Things like pronouncing the letter 'W.' Your 'W' will sound more like a 'V.'"

Grace shifted her relatively heavy body in her chair uncomfortably. Her pale, puffy, and round face looked anxious. She ran her fingers through her short and strawberry-blonde hair, and asked, "But is it permanent?"

"Hopefully not. For the majority of cases, the issue is resolved within a few months. But there is a small chance that it might take much longer, and yes, possibly you might not be able to utter 'W' . . . permanently," the doctor replied.

Agha[1] Javad quickly rummaged through his brain to find

[1] "Agha" is added as a preamble/post-amble to name of men in Farsi as a sign of respect. Its equivalent for women is "khanom," which is typically

something depressing enough to think about to suppress his imminent laughter. His intensely labored sadness came out as a comical scowl, like that of a four-year-old working hard to look serious. It did not last long either. The more Agha Javad considered what the doctor had just said, the less he could hold back his laughter. Karma, ruthless and cold-blooded karma, had done him a magnificent and unexpected favor! Karma, who despite all the rumors, rarely if ever avenges the initiators of malice, had assessed his case, and after long hours of deliberation had decided that something had to be done this time! While imagining karma and its masterful performance, Agha Javad forgot to hold back and broke into a childish giggle, laughing till tears ran down his cheeks.

The doctor pressed her thin lips together and with an angry and baffled look stared at Agha Javad. She then turned her gaze toward Grace. But to her surprise, in Grace's face she read the hint of a reason behind her husband's laughter. So she put her hands in her white coat pockets and stared blankly at a point on the clean white wall behind the examination bed where Grace was sitting, and waited for the storm to pass.

2.

On their way back home, Agha Javad and Grace sat beside each other on the orange seats of a Virginia subway train, each thinking of "W" in their own way.

Grace reminisced about her life over the past few years. She thought of the numerous times she had corrected Agha Javad's pronunciations. And then, she remembered the historical and bloody proceedings of "*Jawad v. Javad.*" Her defeat now seemed inevitable.

While holding on to Grace's big, heavy black purse which was resting on his lap, Agha Javad thought about all the words that contained W, and with childish pleasure, mentally pronounced

---

added as a post-amble.

each and every one of those words with W replaced by V: vhich, vhy, velcome, vhat, vhen, vake up, vax . . . Then he looked down at his small shoes, and those of the other passengers on board, hoping to find a pair of men's shoes smaller than his own. When the train moved underground, Agha Javad raised his head and looked at the window on his side. He could see his own reflection in it: a middle-aged man, wearing a vertically striped blue-and-white shirt, one of many almost identical ones he owned. His father used to wear this pattern . . .

He thought about his father, the wrinkles around his eyes, his voice, the way he smoked. His father was a chain smoker. His vertically striped blue-and-white shirts in minutely varying shades were always stuffed with a pack of Bahman cigarettes in their breast pockets next to his Bic black pen. Everything he owned smelled of cigarettes: his house, his sheets, his clothes, his pen . . .

Many years ago, one sunny winter day like today, Agha Javad had said goodbye to his father. Those years, the bloody Iran-Iraq war had come down to the streets of Ahvaz. Agha Javad fled north and took refuge in Tehran together with his first wife Soheila and his six-year-old son Somon, leaving his old widower father behind. He never saw his father again. A little while after he left, his father and his childhood house were bombed to oblivion. The day he heard the news, he went and bought himself multiple vertically striped blue-and-white shirts and started smoking. Throughout the years, no amount of blackened and rotten lung pictures waved at him made Agha Javad love smoking any less. After moving to Tehran, he tried to find a position as a professor of sociology in a university—what he had been doing in Ahvaz. Having no luck in that, for several years after, he worked as a high school teacher, teaching Persian literature. When Somon was twelve, Soheila died of a heart disease. A few years after Soheila's passing, Agha Javad and Somon emigrated to the US.

3.

Agha Javad and Grace both worked at a public office, which recorded and maintained the ownership, boundaries, and plots of public and private real estate in a Virginia county. Although their cubicles were located on two different floors, they both went to the same small chain sandwich shop near their workplace. That was where they met almost five years ago. Aside from being near their office, this particular sandwich shop had the advantage of offering sweet potato fries, a favorite to both.

It was a rainy Thursday in the month of May. Grace had been moving back and forth between her desk and the female restroom on the second floor with her usual soft and undetermined steps. She had tried to fix her gaze at a distant space, just to ensure that it would not tumble into one of her coworkers whom she had tried to befriend not long before.

Meanwhile, on the first floor, Agha Javad had had several random conversations with one or another of his coworkers during which he had struggled to translate Farsi proverbs and poems to English, and had desperately searched for English equivalents of Farsi words. He had just come up with new caustic words of wisdom the night before during a phone conversation with his son, and had found a way to show it off to his coworkers: "You see, my friend! Optimism is like feeling comfortable with a black toilet seat in a public bathroom."

For a long time, Agha Javad and Grace had sat at adjacent tables in their favorite sandwich shop, each eating their respective sandwiches and sweet potatoes in isolation, without exchanging a word. Then, that Thursday noon after Agha Javad received his sandwich and sweet potato order, the man behind the counter informed Grace, who was standing in a parallel line, that there were no more sweet potatoes left for the day. It had been a depressing week for Grace. She felt very weary. The night before she had sat at her kitchen table till late through the night, drinking herbal tea and reading glossy magazines. She had flipped through them, and had paused often to stare at the pictures of the women on some pages. She had examined herself on her phone's camera, straightening her shoulders, lifting her chin, working out her facial muscles, and then had felt a heavy, sweaty and clumsy numbness run through her arms and legs, a numbness that had lingered in her legs even as she stood in the line at the sandwich shop the next day. She had read a few of the articles with promising titles, and had tried hard to derive a deep, meaningful and practical life lesson, something that could shake up her life dramatically. But nothing seemed to withstand the gravity of her own inadequacies.

"You can have my sweet potatoes if you wish!"

Grace looked up and stared at Agha Javad for a few seconds. She tried hard to pull herself out of the fog of her gloomy thoughts. Eventually she processed the words uttered by Agha Javad.

"That's kind of you. But no, thanks."

"How about sharing?" Agha Javad offered in a scratchy voice and heavy Farsi accent.

Grace looked at him again. He was small, deeply tanned, and had black curly hair. His nose was hooked, almost resembling an eagle's beak. Even his glowing black eyes were reminiscent of an eagle's. They looked unreadable and distant.

Agha Javad and Grace chose a small round table among the remaining empty small round tables. The table they found most suitable was a little unstable and had some leftover crumbs on its surface. They each cleaned the table with a napkin, and when they were happy with the result, they smiled at each other. Then, they sat, and in between their strenuous mental efforts to come up with things to talk about, ate their sandwiches and shared sweet potatoes. As they walked back to their office, Grace thought about the prospects of dating Agha Javad, an attractive Middle-Eastern man, far from his home, who spent as much labor uttering English words as one might when axing a tree, whose accent and limited English prevented him from accessing many concepts in English, and a faint smile brightened her pale face, and creased the corners of her eyes. She felt the opening of a new horizon—a horizon of an unknown, yet new, exciting, and liberating world, in which she believed she no longer had to suffer for her mediocrity.

From that day on, Agha Javad and Grace met at noon on the first floor of their building and walked together to the sandwich shop. During their walks, Agha Javad mostly stared at his small, black leather shoes, and Grace at a not very distant point ahead. Although they both tried hard to find something to say to one another, most of their steps were taken in unsettling silence.

Five months after the day they shared sweet potato fries, Agha Javad and Grace got married. The day after that, Grace moved in with Agha Javad.

Since the day Soheila died, Agha Javad had always known he wanted to remarry. He liked the routine of married life. But he was not one of those people to whom love comes easily, not because he was picky, but because he had no specific requirements for "the" one, or in his case "one". Essentially, all single females in his age range met his requirements. Sadly, and unbeknownst to him, his unconditionally open invitation for love was the exact reasons why most women dismissed it. It was as if Agha Javad applied justice to the one single area in which nobody demanded it.

Despite all this, for some reason, Soheila did take him up on his offer, and years later so did Grace.

Agha Javad and Grace's shared life did not turn out as romance novels professed. Their lives were connected together with feeble strings, as frail and fragile as a sweet potato fry.

Alas, once you open a door, embrace a lover, or shelter a stranger, the story does not end. It does not end with a lugubrious smile, or a heart filled with hope for better days. It reveals its true face the day after—the day after fleeing chaos and seeking refuge in a new land, the day after opening the door to a stranger, a new lover, once the sun comes up.

Agha Javad and Grace's married life mostly consisted of solitary routines. Every night Agha Javad left for a long walk around the neighborhood. During his walks, he reminisced over Soheila, their old house in Ahvaz, their fleeing the war, and their life in Tehran. He felt agitated over his son, Somon. He was worried about Somon's studies, his identity crisis as an Iranian immigrant, and his homesickness. He wished he could cover Somon's ears from the cruel words he would inevitably hear. He had tried for long to shelter him. When he wasn't thinking about these things, Agha Javad ruminated over philosophical problems and in his head discerned sociological patterns and theorized them.

Grace too continued her relentless search for a "solution" among the pages of glossy magazines as she drank herbal tea, only that perhaps now she felt slightly less gloomy. She did have beautiful long fingers that in another world could have made her a dexterous pianist. Her blood tests too always made her proud. Her skin was great, and more importantly, she was open-minded and generous for, "unlike others," not caring about Agha Javad's race and color.

The biggest thing Grace and Agha Javad shared was the contentment they found in simple pleasures they had both held on to since childhood. Perhaps it was relying on this shared feeling that despite the deep chasm between their worlds, they shared some good moments together. There were, for instance, the times when Agha Javad and Grace would sit at their round kitchen table and eat Iranian food he had made them, when the house was rich with the smell of fried onions and saffron, and their hearts with something close to love. Or the few hours after dinner, when they would turn on the TV, each sit at their designated spot on the couch, stretch their legs in comfort, and know that neither of them was looking for anything in the outside world beyond the windows in the darkness, and a sense of security and serenity would envelop them like a velvety blanket. Or the weekday mornings when they got in the car, each holding a cup of coffee in their hands, heading to their shared work place, with the smell of roasted coffee filling their nostrils, giving them solace.

4.

On the first day they had shared sweet potato fries, Agha Javad had attempted to correct Grace using what he believed to be a memorable example: "You see, I am Javad with a V instead of a W. Think of V like vegetable. When you call me, think of vegetables!" And Grace had laughed and thought of a bowl full of steamed broccoli. But as time passed, Grace learned to reflect her discontent with her husband in converting his name back to Jawad. Most of her discontent stemmed from barely ever receiving a compliment, or even a word of encouragement from her husband. What she did not know was that this characteristic was not specific to Agha Javad, but rather a cultural phenomenon, common to many men around Agha Javad's age and origin. So their battles over Jawad v. Javad continued and eventually grew sour and bloody. The more Grace felt frustrated with not receiving any sort of approval or encouragement about herself from her husband, the higher the frequency with which she reverted to Jawad. And the more frequent this reversion, the fewer reasons Agha Javad found to feel kindly toward Grace, let alone give her compliments.

This war reached its pinnacle last year during their Thanksgiving dinner. That night, they were hosting Grace's parents, her sister and brother-in-law, and Somon, when asking Agha Javad to pass the dish of steamed vegetables, Grace once again addressed him as "Jawad". Passing the dish, Agha Javad pointed at the steamed vegetables and said a bit irritably, "After five years, do I *still* have to remind you: V like vegetable?"

But that night Grace was not in the mood to compromise. Her inner voice was very loud, echoing in her ears a sentence she had borrowed from one of her glossy magazines: *You know what you want and you go for it!*

So, in response to Agha Javad's complaint, she clarified,

"Recently a new coworker has joined our office on my floor, an Arab lady, from, from I think Egypt, yes, Egypt. She told me that her brother's name is Jawad too. She told me that Jawad is an Arabic name, and that is how it is pronounced: Ja-Wad, Ja-Wad!"

Agha Javad and Grace stared at each other for a few seconds.

Then, Agha Javad directed his stare at the guests sitting at the dinner table. He paused on each guest for a while, as if to ensure they were all aware of the crime that had just been committed.

Then he explained, "Just like you guys pronounce Khashayarsha as 'Xerxes' in English, we pronounce Jawad as Javad in Farsi! Okay?"

Agha Javad had intended to make this statement with patience, while wearing a smile of generosity. But instead, he uttered it forcefully and emotionally, while his face and ears flushed and his heartbeat spiked.

Grace, who in that specific moment was very sure of her right to assert any of her personal ideas with conviction, responded nonchalantly, "You know, a dialect is different from a language. In a big country, for instance, there may be people who speak the same language, but in different dialects."

"So?" Agha Javad replied.

"So, maybe in your dialect they pronounce Jawad as Javad. But in your language, the correct pronunciation is actually Jawad!"

"My dialect? My dialect? What do you know about my dialect?" answered Agha Javad.

"Farsi! Your dialect is Farsi!" replied Grace quickly.

Agha Javad felt livid. Every circuit in his brain sparked, each urging a different response. But in the end, tired of the most futile discussion in the world, in a slow, weary, and exasperated voice, he addressed the people around the dinner table. "Vegetable. All I asked from you people was this. One simple vegetable. And *that* seems to have been too much to ask for!"

He then threw his napkin on the floor, rose up, and left the room.

Grace bit her lower lip and looked at Agha Javad's empty chair. A few seconds later, when she tried to collect herself and appear graceful and calm, she felt a sudden rush of depression. She slowly moved her bangs behind her ears and stared at the various dishes she had spent all that day and the prior day preparing. Then her eyes fell upon the china bowl full of steamed vegetables, and whispered, "V like vegetable! V like vegetable!"

5.

The train was shaking, and with it the bodies of the passengers. Grace and Agha Javad had both zoned out of time and place. After some time they looked at each other, not sure of what the future held, or how they felt.

Agha Javad studied Grace. Her eyes looked sad and puffy. The two sides of her lips had moved downward, as if to sketch an upside down V. Her soft hands with their beautiful, long fingers were placed tidily on her big, wide thighs. In her posture there was something like an acquiescence to insurmountable forces. Something bearing the semblance of giving in to the sea, whose waves grow bigger and bigger and the ground underneath deeper and deeper. And then, gradually, there are only the loud sounds of waves, and the softness of water, and then . . . nothingness.

Agha Javad felt his heart squeeze. The train was moving above ground, and a hot and an intense sun was beaming in. As he stared at the sun dust dancing in the light, he remembered the hot sun of Ahvaz on the day he and Soheila were loading all their bags and suitcases into their old yellow Peykan[1], the day they fled the war together with Somon. How numb and heavy his legs had felt, and how the rush of reality had cleared all questions he had ever had about how people feel when calamity befalls them.

Suddenly, a strong sense of pity seized Agha Javad's heart—pity for himself, for Somon, for Soheila, and for Grace. For all

---

1 A specific make of car, which was the most widely used vehicle in Iran between the years 1970 and 2000.

that they had to endure, and for all they felt urged to impose onto others—just to serve their desire for a little bit of dignity. What a disastrous desire. What a fragile and vulnerable feeling dignity is. It might as well be the biggest incongruity of Homo sapiens—a mortal and needy, class-conscious, xenophobic, violent, yet vulnerable creature who herself could not endure what she imposes on others of her kind.

Agha Javad firmed his grip on Grace's purse. Then he asked Grace, who was staring straight ahead, almost motionless, "What do you say we get off at the next stop? There is a bookstore around there. For the first few years after Somon and I had immigrated, we would sit in that bookstore for long hours every day and stare at people coming and going. I miss that place, and I have heard it is at the brink of bankruptcy. I want to show it to you before it goes under."

Grace did not respond. Her sad and puffy eyes continued to stare ahead. But something in the state of her lips and hands changed. A change that, although almost imperceptible, was not missed by Agha Javad.

Finally, the train stopped at the next station. Grace took her purse from Agha Javad's lap and stood up. Then in a melancholy yet resolute voice, she called, "Let's go, Javad. Let's go."

BAIT BALL

A dense, spherical shoal of small fish who spin in unison as a defense against predators

You want to believe the mantra *There's safety in numbers*
but some count a bomb in a backpack as affirmative
action—by equal opportunity deployment.

You want to believe there's safety when you're herded
through a checkpoint or onto a reservation
but herd animals are unnerved by the cattle guards
and the dimmest pigeon won't perch on razor wire.

We're mostly little fish
counting on our numbers to go up
but the elevator's down and the census taker is tired

so we close ranks into this whirling ball, but
with a hundred seconds till closing on the Doomsday Clock
it's all bait-and-switch, feeding us a line.
We're buying time, swimming for our lives,

dodging phishing scammers, data breachers,
fishy telemarketers with dolphin smiles,
shark-keen robocallers, Moby Dicks.

The net effect: you want to believe
in war *games*, friendly fire, shining seas,
purple mountain majesties, resurrection,
that something shredded can be made great again,

and with all those red herrings swallowed whole,
that frenzied feckless sphere of flailing fish,
in the comforting social security of a bait ball.

ALIENATION

When the alien arrives we will need to prepare
ourselves. Several cultural practices will be confused.
What portions of its body should be
covered out in public, for example.
Imperative will be gender assignation.

When the alien arrives we will have to refine
the pecking order. Should we bow or curtsy,
shake hands, cheek peck, fist bump, or Thai wai—
but all these forms presume anatomy.
Paramount will be this determination.

When the alien arrives we will be forced to redefine
"fellow" creature (gender notwithstanding).
If a human is a person and a person must be human . . .
To this tautology if we add exobiology
we can be sure to avoid discrimination.

When the alien arrives we will need to address
the dignitary—business letter etiquette, high priority.
But, as to *its* business, en"Dear"ment may be
premature. And honorifics—what if "Lord" or "God"?
We must surrender the appropriate combination.

When the aliens arrive we will try to convert them
to our ways. Teach them our language, culture, holy texts,
technology. Gift them trinkets, another Golden Record.

They tour us through their starship, inscrutable
as monks. (So much for the question of domination.)

As the aliens arrive we will try to curtail
interaction. Our firm position remains: missionary
urges must be quelled. Curiosity
about heavenly bodies only breeds
the highest threat of all—miscegenation.

Once the aliens arrive we should plan to acquire
someone's land (eminent domain, global scale).
If assimilation and extermination fail,
coexistence may require the last solution:
founding of the first alien nation.

At the Musée d'Orsay, my granddad stood laughing in front of a portrait of a nude woman resting on a chaise lounge.

Kate Carmody

FAMILY PIECE

My Uber driver to my friends' Halloween party is Cuban. I tell him my granddad is Cuban. He says, "No English. Sorry." I check Google Translate to make sure I'm correct and then say, "Mi abuelo es Cubano." He tells me something, and I have to say, "Lo siento. No hablo Español." I want to tell him about my trip to Cuba. I want to ask what brought him to Denver. But can't. We sit in silence for the rest of the twenty-minute ride. He doesn't even turn on the radio. I don't even check my phone. I just stare out the window. When we get to my friends' house, I say, "Gracias por todo," and close the door.

My granddad's full name was René Antonio Eulogio Amado Jesus de la Caridad Torrado y Pruna, but he left everything in Cuba except Rene and Torrado, including his parents. When Castro took control, he urged them to move to Miami. "What's one more dictator?" Abuela said.

Castro's men showed up at my great-grandmother's door while her husband Rudolfo was out. They tied Abuela to a chair and gagged her while ransacking the place. "If we find one gun," they threatened, "we'll kill you." She prayed they wouldn't search the barn. They didn't. I imagine soldiers stuffing things in their pockets as they searched. I imagine them taunting her as she watched, tied to her chair.

At the Musée d'Orsay, my granddad stood laughing in front of a portrait of a nude woman resting on a chaise lounge. "It was this same woman, except she was facing the other way," he said, referring to the Renoir painting he left in Cuba. The only thing I ever heard him regret leaving behind. "So many times I wanted to bring it back. I always said, 'I'll get it next time.' Now it's in one of Fidel's mansions."

June 4, 1970, Abuela and Rodolfo landed in Miami on a Freedom Flight as political asylum seekers with "nothing but the clothes on their backs and ten cents in their pockets," I was told. But Rodolfo Guzman, polo player and entrepreneur, was no longer the man that everyone in Cuba recognized. "He died of a broken heart," my granddad said. He missed his horses.

On Ancestry.com, I found records of Abuela's visits to my granddad in medical school at Tulane before the Revolution, before they lost everything, before my granddad lost "y Pruna."

Abuela wanted Granddad to come back to Cuba after medical school, but he fell in love with the United States. After his residency in Texas, he moved to Miami. November 12, 1940, the day before his twenty-eighth birthday, he became a naturalized citizen.

My granddad enlisted in the Navy the day after Pearl Harbor but couldn't join because he hadn't been a citizen long enough. He joined the Army instead. A couple of months later, he and his surgical team shipped off to England and eventually to Normandy.

Granddad spoke Spanish, English, French, Italian, and German. I can speak English. "Cómo está usted?" I'd proudly say as a kid. "Muy bien, gracias. ¿Y tú?" I'd answer before anyone had a chance to. And if someone asked me, "¿Habla Español?" I knew to say, "Un poco." But, really, I don't know Spanish, not even a little, not even after two years of Spanish in high school. My granddad would call and speak in Spanish when I answered. "I'm sorry, Granddad, but I don't know what that means yet," I'd say, waiting for his disappointment to reach me. "Why aren't you learning anything? Don't you care about where I came from?" I did. I do.

"I don't really consider myself Hispanic or Latina. I don't focus on being Cuban, or Scottish or English on my mom's side for that matter. I consider myself American. We grew up American," my mom said. "Caring about your heritage is a Midwest thing. I never even knew people cared about that stuff until I got to college, and everyone would talk about how Irish, German, or Italian they were. People assumed I was Italian."

I never thought of myself as Hispanic and Latina until I started checking boxes to classify myself as such for college admissions. My aunt said it could help with acceptance. Because of my 3.2 GPA and ADHD struggles with school, I assumed colleges accepted me because of my ethnicity. When I started getting invitations to Latinx student events, I felt guilty for taking the place of someone more Latina than me.

Every once in a while, my mom and I decide we want to learn Spanish. I thought Granddad didn't teach his kids Spanish because he was focused on being American. I thought maybe he'd lost his culture in the melting pot. But my mom said her father never spoke Spanish around the house because my grandmother Mimi didn't speak it. "Any Spanish I knew, I learned from the maids," my mom said.

"Your father has been practicing his French for weeks," my mother said before our trip to France. "He should know enough to help us get around." *Doesn't Granddad know French?* My granddad thought he was too old to remember. When we got to

Paris, my dad was surprised at how little he'd retained, and my 92-year-old granddad became our translator.

When his health was declining, Granddad sometimes forgot to speak in English. His wife, Diane, told him she couldn't help him because she didn't speak Spanish. She knew un poco. They lived in Miami, where most people know a little Spanish. According to a medical journal, "In the elderly retreat to a primary language may be an early indicator for development of cognitive decline or dementia."[1] His wife was a nurse.

Granddad urgently repeated several stories. "When I went to boarding school in Baltimore as a kid, I didn't know any English. By Christmas," he'd remind us, "I could speak English as well as I can today." When I got older, I asked my mom if it was true. "That seems unlikely, but it could be. I don't know. You never know with Dad. He has a photographic memory, so it may be true." He'd continue: "Some kid called me a spic once, and I beat the crap out of him. Then, no one ever called me a spic again." I'd never heard the word "spic" the first time he told that story.

The most probable theory about the word *spic* is that it originated when Americans went to Panama to build the canal. According to a *Univision* article, "As the journalist Samuel G. Blythe explained in 1908 in *The Saturday Evening Post*: 'All Americans are alike. They do not bother to learn foreign languages when they go to a foreign country, but they force the natives to learn American.'"[2]

---

1 McMurtray, Aaron, et al. "Language Preference and Development of Dementia Among Bilingual Individuals." *Hawaii Medical Journal*, U.S. National Library of Medicine, Oct. 2009, www.ncbi.nlm.nih.gov/pmc/articles/PMC4335728/.

2 Sánchez Díez, María. "The True Origin of the Word 'Spic,' the Racist Insult Aimed at Hispanics." *Univision*, 14 June 2017, www.univision.com/univision-news/united-states/the-true-origin-of-the-word-spic-the-racist-insult-aimed-at-hispanics.

Americans started calling the Panamanians *Spiggoty* to represent the dialogue between them that began with *Spik d' English* or *No spik d' English. Spiggoty* eventually turned into the derogatory term *spic* and included all Spanish speakers.

Abuela did not speak English. It must have been weird for my mom and her siblings never to speak directly to their grandmother. When I was little, she said something to my granddad in Spanish, and I replied in gibberish, thinking I was speaking Spanish. My mom said Abuela laughed and said something back to me. Then, I'm told, we had a full Spanish/ gibberish conversation at the kitchen table.

My granddad always told me how much I looked like Abuela. "My only Cuban-looking grandchild," he'd say. Of the six grandchildren, I'm the only one with brown eyes. I didn't see a resemblance, but whenever he said that, it made me feel special.

Since most of the hotels and resorts are state-run, my partner and I booked casa particulares for our visit to Cuba. Casa particular translates to "private house" in English, which means we rented rooms from Cuban residents versus the government. The host of our casa particular in Havana arranged a friend to pick us up from José Martí International Airport. On our way to the apartment, the driver asked in English what brought us to Havana. "Don't tell anyone you're Cuban," my family said, "They may not let you come back." I decided to let Justin answer and resisted telling them about our plans to retrace my grandfather's past. After Justin said that he's a musician and fan of Cuban music, our driver started making suggestions about places to go and invited us to see his band perform at the cultural center that night.

A couple of hours later, he picked us up. While his band set up, Justin and I walked to a nearby restaurant. I found an open table while Justin ordered at the counter. An older woman with a plate of food sat down across from me at the picnic table. "Buenos noches," she said and smiled. *Buenos noches.* She took a bite of her food. Then, said something else to me. *Lo siento. No hablo Español.* She seemed surprised. "¿No?" And probably disappointed. *No. Lo siento. Lo siento.* She nodded, smiled, and started talking to the man behind her as she ate. I waited for Justin. She turned back. Ate a few more bites. I fumbled through my backpack and grabbed some gum. "American?" *Sí.* "Ah sí," she said and nodded. I smiled. She smiled back. I looked to see if Justin was coming back. He wasn't. I popped a piece of gum out of the foil. She looked down at it. I wanted to offer her a piece but didn't know how. I looked to see if Justin was coming, so he could translate. He wasn't. I pointed to the gum and then to her. She smiled and thanked me. I handed her the pack of gum. She put it in her purse.

The first week of sixth grade at my Catholic elementary school in St. Louis, my teacher told us to draw a picture representing our family's heritage as a "getting-to-know-you" activity. I drew Irish and German flags to represent my dad's side and the British and Cuban flags to represent my mom's. My teacher hung our pictures in the classroom. Irish and German flags were on many, if not most of the students' drawings, and a few had British flags, but I was the only one with a Cuban flag—a difference I took pride in. I doubt anyone noticed this, considering I didn't look any different from the other white kids in our class.

"Play dead and see who comes to your funeral." Whenever my family talks about Granddad, my aunt and cousin remind us of the sayings he repeated. My cousin's favorite is "To eat fish and tell lies, one must be careful." Mine is "No Latin ever killed himself over a skinny woman." I'm told there are dozens more.

But those are the only ones I remember. I'm not sure if he learned them in Cuba, here, or if he invented them. I typed a few into my search engine, but nothing came up. My aunt Carmen said she once made a list of all his aphorisms, but I've never seen it. It's on a computer she doesn't use anymore.

A year or so after Rodolfo and Abuela settled into their apartment in Hialeah, there was a knock at the door. A man handed Abuela a bag, she thanked him, and he left. Abuela opened the bag and carefully checked each item. Most of the jewelry she paid him to smuggle into the US was there. She was grateful to see any of it. She and Rodolfo, now in their late seventies, will sell some of the pieces, including one of her five karat diamond earrings. The other earring will be used to pay for her only son's medical care at the end of his life. Another diamond piece will be given to Abuela's grandson to start his home hospice care business. She will give her two 1915 gold Cuban coin rings to her granddaughters, Carmen and Suzzie. Suzzie will give her ring to her daughter, Kate, on her thirtieth birthday, and she will wear it every day.

While watching the Netflix documentary series *The Cuba Libre Story*, I learned that the man on my coin ring is the Cuban poet, essayist, and patriot José Martí.

"I'm not a hero; I just took care of a lot of heroes," my granddad said at the end of Carmen's filmed interview with him.

Next to my name in my granddad's will, it states, "the World War II memories of my Service so that she has the material necessary for the book she wants to write."

> June 6—1944—D-Day! How can I ever forget this horrible day! From the beginning it was obvious

that the Jerries were fighting desperately & taking a terrific toll on our men and equipment. We left the transport area at 08:00, and were due to land by 10:30. We were in a rhino-ferry. We never got to land that day. Four times we attempted, & were refused. Once they had us pinned down with the .88 guns, that only God could have spared us, and did. We had casualties on board. With one of our engines knocked out, we finally headed to one of the LST's and tied alongside. As soon as darkness ensued, enter the German planes giving us hell. We were strafed 3 times. I dived under a 2 ½ ton truck filled with explosives. All during the nite, the Navy kept bombarding the beach trying to locate the 88's. Finally, I fell asleep under the truck. I woke up the next day—

June 7—'44, with water lapping up. Al Brocere & I climbed up to the LST, got coffee and cereal, and found that we were going to make another try at landing, this time by LCVP. The idea was better, so our team, Campbell's team & William's, boarded the craft and made for the beach which was still under fire. We got about 30 yards off shore & had to swim the rest in. That channel water was cold. We saw a Red Cross on top of the hill, & made for it, finding it to be the clearing station of the 1st Medical Battalion where I dried my clothes & got to work, as there were many casualties. We had no equipment of our own, so we could not set up. In the afternoon, we moved to another station, just outside of St. Laurent sur Mer. It was another hot spot, with shelling, and

> the added hazard of sniping with the snipers not respecting our Red Cross. We worked until past mid-nite, I finally went to sleep in one of the trucks, as I had not had time to dig a fox hole.

In the Normandy American Cemetery and Memorial, I filmed the rows of white crosses with Stars of David scattered amongst them. I took photographs of graves with fresh flowers resting on them. And a few more of another that reads, "HERE RESTS IN HONORED GLORY A COMRADE IN ARMS KNOWN BUT TO GOD."

I'm re-watching the documentary I made from our trip to Normandy. We're at a café after visiting the Normandy American Cemetery and Memorial. My brother Patrick asks my granddad, "How did you swim to shore? I thought you weren't a great swimmer." Granddad laughs. "I still don't know how. The water was colder than hell," he says. "Were there bodies in the water?" He leans in closer to Patrick. "What was that?" Perhaps slightly surprised by my brother's question, perhaps struggling to hear in the loud café. "Were there a lot of bodies?" Patrick asks louder directly in his good ear. Granddad nods. Perhaps feeling his scotch enough to answer as a person and not as a historian or surgeon. He says, "That's the thing that I've dreamed about many times." *You dream about it?* I ask behind the camera. He nods again and hangs his head for a moment, repositioning the napkin in his lap. He picks his head up and stares at the camera. "That would be kinda scary," Patrick says. Granddad stays fixated on the camera. Then, looks away. "Do you ever dream about it now, Dad?" My mom asks off-camera. "Huh?" She repeats the question louder. Granddad nods more emphatically. He turns to her. "It's funny for years I didn't. Then, the last four or five years . . . at least two or three times, I always have the same dream of the bodies floating on the water." His hands motion forward with invisible bodies. He focuses on my camera again, raises his eyebrows, frowns, then looks down at the table.

When my family visited Omaha Beach, where my granddad and the Allies landed, it was low tide like it was on D-Day. Patrick wanted to get a sense of what it would have been like for the soldiers. Halfway to the ocean, he stopped to take a picture. I took a picture of my brother, a toy soldier in the distance, the capping waves nowhere near close enough to pull him from his position.

Many soldiers never made it to the beach. Their fight was with the Channel and ninety pounds of gear weighing them down.

As a kid, I got caught in a wave in Lake Michigan. I've been afraid of drowning ever since.

Standing on the wall at the base of the bluffs in Normandy was the only time I've ever been in awe of the enormity of a beach, the only time I've realized a beach can also swallow you.

"The only time I ever felt ashamed to be American," my granddad would say, "was with that Elián González fiasco." He'd cross his arms, shake his head, and scowl. Fishermen found Elián clinging to an inner tube a few miles off the coast of Fort Lauderdale on Thanksgiving Day, 1999. His mother and her boyfriend had drowned when their boat capsized on their journey to the United States. Cuban exiles in the States urged our government to let him stay while his father and folks back home fought for his return. I remember feeling sorry for the boy caught up in the spectacle, too young to decide on his own. Months later, Elián's relatives in Miami were instructed to return him to his father, who would bring him back to Havana. When they refused, Janet

Reno led the charge in raiding their home. A photographer was there to capture an immigration officer in SWAT gear with an assault rifle in the screaming face of Elián holding tightly to his uncle. Years later, my granddad was still angry about it. "It was absolutely horrible." Granddad was disgusted by the thought of a child being plucked from freedom, from the arms of a loved one at gunpoint by our government and put into the arms of the regime that took everything from our family at gunpoint.

> 8 June—'44, We live in fox holes, have not bathed or washed for 3 days, and we work incessantly. We are all getting more than our share of surgery. Gradually we are getting used to the noise of battle, and we find that the best antidote for fear is work. We hear our troops are doing O.K. Although we are in the show, we know little or nothing of the weapon of the war.

Most Christmases Granddad would come to St. Louis. When I was in high school, we went to Miami. We spent Christmas Eve with Granddad and the Cuban side of the family. It was the first and only time I've celebrated Noche Buena. It was the first time I was old enough to remember our exchanges. We ate roasted pork, black beans, rice, fried plantains, and flan. My sister and I started talking to my granddad's cousin David. "What was it like in Cuba after the Revolution?" my sister asked. My sister Ryann was (and still is) always good at asking the questions I was afraid to. "It was very hard. They didn't allow professionals to leave the country," he said. "I'm a mechanical engineer, and my wife is a pharmacy doctor." As David started to explain rationing, he put his fists together. "They would give you a chicken this big for the week for your entire family." He stuck his fists out in front of us.

Justin and I bought our flight to Havana shortly after commercial flights to Cuba resumed in the fall of 2016, and shortly before Trump took office. We put together a binder of research on my family, a detailed itinerary, and places to check out. We started planning around the addresses I got from boat and flight manifests in Ancestry. I'd found the addresses of three homes in two different neighborhoods—two apartments in Vedado, one house in Miramar—from three decades of Granddad's and Abuela's travels between Cuba and the US. Justin and I figured out approximate locations of each place on a street map and used Cuba guidebooks to learn about the neighborhoods pre- and post-Castro. Of the homes mentioned in my granddad's stories, the farm's address was missing from the manifests. My mom suggested asking Granddad's cousin David. I got his number from my uncle Drake, who warned me he might not be pleased about me going to Cuba.

I called David a week before our trip. I said my partner and I were going to Cuba to do research for my book, and I wanted to ask him some questions before I visited places where he grew up. "I don't know if you are going to find something that is similar to the way it was before Castro," he said. "When I left—I left thirty-seven years ago—everything was destroyed." He said maybe they renovated places for the tourists, but he didn't know because he hasn't gone back. I asked David about the farm. He said it was more of a polo club than a farm. David lived there with his wife and daughter. "They came knocking on the door of the farm and put machine guns against us and said we have weapons here." He said they didn't, but it didn't matter. The last time he drove by the polo farm was in 1977. After the government seized the land, they kept the stable and turned the house into a slab of concrete. "After that, I never went back. I didn't want to." I wondered if I should be visiting a place that caused my family so much pain, a place that, unlike Normandy, has nothing to memorialize their suffering.

Justin and I spent the last two nights of our Cuba trip in the Miramar neighborhood. We tried to get a place close to the address we had for my granddad's home on Avenida Quinta or Fifth Avenue. Besides the farm, I'd heard the most about the house in Miramar. It was the one my mom and uncle René Jr. visited as kids. The apartments in Vedado were new discoveries, neither my mom nor granddad ever mentioned them. But the house in Miramar, my granddad or mom or aunt or uncles would always say, "is now, I heard, the Japanese Embassy."

Justin and I hailed a taxi and asked the driver to take us to the Japanese Embassy. Much of this day is foggy. Like every other day in Cuba, we started the day with expectations from what we learned before our trip combined with no idea what to expect. When we stayed in Vedado, we noticed that the old mansions that had a touch-up of paint were government buildings, schools, restaurants, and clubs. Some more recently updated than others. Some mansions were private residences with fenced-in yards and guards on duty. Others were private residences with multiple families living in them. Many of the mansions occupied by everyday Cubans were visibly crumbling as they were in other parts of the city. Among the renovated and decrepit mansions on palm tree-lined blocks were properties with nothing but a pile of rubble. I wondered what was there before and felt sorry for the families who didn't have the means to repair their homes, but what I felt in Miramar was different. And that feeling is what makes my memory foggy.

I remember the taxi driver said that cars aren't allowed to go below a certain speed limit or stop on Avenida Quinta because of all the foreign embassies. We asked him to get us as close as possible. I remember finding the Japanese Embassy in an office-style building and hearing from someone that the Embassy had not always been in that building, so it could have been in one of the mansions before. The person said we could ask the US Embassy for records of past embassy addresses, but we'd have to wait until Monday since it was Saturday.

I took out Granddad's address. I wasn't sure if the streets' addresses or the houses' had changed since the Revolution. We started walking, looking for a mid-century modern home that resembled the one from the photograph of the house a relative took while visiting Cuba a few years before. I remember the trimmed trees, hedges, and grass as we walked down the parkway of the four-lane street lined with an impressive mixture of art deco, modern, and neoclassical homes. But I didn't waste time gawking. Justin looked for the address on the left, and I looked on the right. "I wish I would've thought to ask the Embassy before," I said. "What if we came all this way and can't find it?" Justin reassured me that we'd find it. "We should have come here on the first day."

We walked briskly down the parkway scanning the homes and hotels. Wi-Fi services were limited to certain areas, which meant we couldn't plug in the address for directions. All we had was the map we'd bought in Denver and an offline street guide app.

We finally reached the address. I stared at it through the chain-linked fence, trying to figure out if it was the same as what I'd seen. Black mold crawled up the stone columns framing the windows. Chunks of the flat red roof were missing, and in other areas, the roof's rust bled onto the off-white exterior. The house was broken up into two apartments: one on top and one on the bottom. I couldn't tell if it was built that way. "Is this it?" Justin asked. "I don't know," I said quietly. Even with the photo, it looked nothing like what I'd pictured. It wasn't in terrible condition, but it wasn't what I imagined.

As we were taking pictures, a woman walked out onto the upstairs balcony above the garage and started sweeping. "What should we do?" I shrugged my shoulders. "Is that a casa particular sign?" He pointed to the window. The woman noticed us and stopped sweeping. "I think it is. Should we ask if it's available?" Justin asked, moving towards the driveway. "Wait. Justin—I don't know if that's a good idea. What if—" He assured me it was okay. Before I said anything else, he was talking to the woman. I stood at the end of the driveway. He pointed to me. They both looked at me and waved me over. She went back inside, and we walked up the stairs to a side door. "Justin, what are we doing? I don't want them to be suspicious of us." She started opening the door. "It's fine. I said we were looking for a room and saw their sign." She welcomed us in, I said the usual: *Hola. No hablo Español,* and she ushered us into the room for rent.

The walls and ceiling were cracked and moldy. I tried to casually check my pulse as she spoke to Justin. My heart was beating so quickly, I thought I was going to have to sit down. I focused on my breathing. Water stains bubbled in the ceiling. She pointed to the doorway covered with an old green fiberglass corrugated panel. She pushed it aside to reveal a bathroom. I felt lightheaded and fanned myself. We walked out of the room and down the narrow hallway. She introduced us to the other family members and showed us around the kitchen. There was stuff everywhere. Old stuff. Maybe stuff that belonged to my family. I don't know if it was the heat or the sad state of the place or the fact that none of the people there knew they were living in my granddad's home, but I had to get out.

I knew the family didn't have the money to afford supplies for repairs. The place was clean, and they were welcoming. They were just trying to make a living. I guess I didn't expect Granddad's place in Miramar to be like the dilapidated ones in Vedado. I expected it to be like the other renovated, heavily guarded embassies, diplomat homes, or government official palaces we passed walking down the parkway. Part of me wanted it to be an embassy or the playhouse of one of Castro's goons. That would fit my granddad's narrative better. Stories about his Miramar home came second to D-Day in terms of frequency. And every time his story ended with his house occupied by Japan or some other country willing to defy the US. Not once did he ever think that it may be occupied by an average Cuban family trying to get by with what they had.

Justin thanked the woman, said some things I didn't understand, and she escorted us to the door. When we reached the sidewalk, I turned to face the house again, and the woman had resumed sweeping.

Contributors

Essam M. Al-Jassim is a Saudi writer and translator. For many years, he taught English at Royal Commission schools in Jubail, Saudi Arabia. He received his bachelor's degree in Foreign Languages and Education from King Faisal University, Hofuf. His translations have appeared in a variety of print and online literary Arabic and English journals.

Rahme Al-Mghayzawi is an Omani short-story writer. She holds a Master's degree in Management (MiM). Al-Mghayzawi is a member of the Omani Society for Writers and Literati, and has published three short story collections.

Mark Budman is a first-generation immigrant. His writing has appeared or is forthcoming in *Catapult, Witness, Five Points, Guernica/PEN, American Scholar, Huffington Post, Mississippi Review, Virginia Quarterly,* and elsewhere. His novel *My Life at First Try* was published by Counterpoint Press.

Julie Cadwallader Staub lives and writes near Burlington, Vermont. Her first collection of poems, *Face to Face,* was published by Cascadia Publishing House in 2010, and her second collection, *Wing Over Wing,* was published by Paraclete Press in 2019. Her poem "Milk" won *Hunger Mountain Review*'s 2015 Ruth Stone Poetry Prize, and "Turning" was nominated by *Potomac Review* for the 2019 Pushcart Prize. Julie's poems have been published in various journals, featured on *The Writer's Almanac,* and included in anthologies including *Poetry of Presence: An Anthology of Mindfulness Poems* by Grayson Books and *Roads Taken: Contemporary Vermont Poetry* by Green Writers Press.

Kate Carmody's work has appeared in *Essay Daily, No Contact, Los Angeles Review, The Journal of Compressed Creative Arts,* and *Lunch Ticket,* among others. She received her M.F.A. from Antioch University in Los Angeles and teaches writing courses nationally. She is the recipient of a CINTAS Foundations grant supporting artists born in Cuba or of Cuban descent. "Family Piece" is an excerpt from her book-length essay in progress.

Mary Crow is a translator as well as a poet. Her most recent book of poems is *Addicted to the Horizon* and of translations is *Vertical Poetry: Last Poems by Roberto Juarroz.*

Adam Day is the author of *Left-Handed Wolf* (LSU Press, 2020) and *Model of a City in Civil War* (Sarabande Books). He is the recipient of a Poetry Society of America Chapbook Fellowship for Badger, Apocrypha, and of a PEN Award. He is the editor of the forthcoming anthology, *Divine Orphans of the Poetic Project,* from 1913 Press, and he is the publisher of the cultural magazine, *Action, Spectacle.*

Vernita Hall is the author of *Where William Walked: Poems About Philadelphia and Its People of Color,* winner of the Willow Books Grand Prize and of the Robert Creeley Prize from Marsh Hawk Press; and *The Hitchhiking Robot Learns About Philadelphians,* winner of the Moonstone Press Chapbook Contest. Her poems have appeared or are forthcoming in numerous anthologies and journals, including *American Poetry Review, African American Review, Atlanta Review, Barrow Street, Baltimore Review, Mezzo Cammin, Solstice,* and *The Cortland Review.* With fellowships from the Fine Arts Work Center and Ucross, Hall holds an M.F.A. in Creative Writing from Rosemont College and serves on the poetry review board of Philadelphia Stories.

Jane Hegstrom is currently working on memoir pieces about her midwestern childhood in the mid-1950s and a collection of essays on aging. She is a graduate of the Masters of Writing Program at Johns Hopkins University. Her writing has appeared in *Bookends Review, Little Patuxent Review, BoomerLit, 5x5,* and *Flint Hills Review.* Jane has a Ph.D. in sociology with a specialization in social psychology and gender. Her academic writing has appeared in *Sex Roles, Discourse Analysis: A Multidisciplinary Journal,* and *Women's Studies: An Interdisciplinary Journal.*

Joshua Jones lives in Maryland, and his writing has appeared in *The Best Microfictions 2020, The Best Small Fictions 2019, The Cincinnati Review, CRAFT, Paper Darts, SmokeLong Quarterly, Split Lip Magazine,* and elsewhere.

Anu Kandikuppa's essays, flash fiction, and short stories have appeared or will appear in *Calyx, Epiphany, Michigan Quarterly Review, The Cincinnati Review (miCRo), The Normal School, The Rumpus,* and other journals, and have received multiple Pushcart Prize and Best of the Net nominations. Anu holds an M.F.A. from the Program for Writers at Warren Wilson College and worked as an economics consultant in a former life. She lives in Boston.

Mehdi M. Kashani lives and writes in Toronto, Canada. His fiction has recently appeared in *Epiphany, EVENT, Bellevue Literary Review,* and *Zone 3,* among others. To learn more about him, visit his website: www.mehdimkashani.com.

Michael Kleber-Diggs is a poet, essayist, and literary critic. His debut poetry collection, *Worldly Things,* won the Max Ritvo Poetry Prize and will be published by Milkweed Editions in June 2021. Michael's work has been supported by the Minnesota State Arts Board and the

Jerome Foundation. He lives in St. Paul, Minnesota, with his wife Karen. They have one child (Elinor), currently away at college pursuing a B.F.A. in Dance Performance, two cats (Curly and Mocha), and two golden doodles (Jasper and Ziggy).

Gloria G. Murray is a member of Poets & Writers, Inc. Her poetry and prose have appeared in journals including *The Paterson Review, Poet Lore, Bardic Echoes, Third Wednesday, Adelaide, Dash, Flapperhouse,* and others. She is the winner of the 2014 first prize Anna Davidson Rosenberg award, *Poetica Magazine,* as well as third prize recipient of the 2017 *Writer's Digest* Poetry contest.

Azin Neishaboori was born and raised in Iran. In 2003, after finishing college, she moved to the U.S. to attend Penn State University, where she received her Ph.D. in Electrical Engineering. Her works of fiction have appeared in *Bellevue Literary Review, Oyster River Pages, Eclectica,* and *The Deadly Writers Patrol.* In her writing, she aspires to challenge the prevalent narrative and hopes to share an authentic and non-politicized perspective of Iranians and other Middle Easterners with the readers.

Richard Prins is a lifelong New Yorker. Publications include *Gulf Coast, jubilat, Ploughshares,* and notable mentions in *Best American Essays* and *Best American Travel Writing.* Arrests include criminal trespass (Trump Tower), disorderly conduct (Trump International Hotel), resisting arrest (Republican National Convention), and incommoding the halls of Congress (United States Senate).

Chloe Chun Seim is a writer living in Lawrence, Kansas. Her work has appeared or is forthcoming in *Yemassee, Hobart, North American Review, Masters Review,* and other publications. Her short story collection has been named a finalist for the 2020 St. Lawrence Book Award, and she received the 2019 Best Heartland Screenplay from Kansas City Women in Film and TV. She holds an M.F.A. from the University of Missouri-Kansas City.

S. Shaw is a librarian for an urban West Coast public library. His poems have been published in *African American Review*, *Temenos Literary Journal*, and *Split This Rock*, with poems upcoming in *The Rhino Poetry Journal*. He is a Cave Canem Poetry Fellow. His chapbook *The House of Men* was published in 2019.

Jane Zwart teaches English at Calvin University, where she also co-directs the Calvin Center for Faith & Writing. Her poems have previously appeared or are forthcoming in *Poetry*, *Ploughshares*, *Threepenny Review*, *The Poetry Review* (UK), and *TriQuarterly*.

www.ingramcontent.com/pod-product-compliance
Lightning Source LLC
Chambersburg PA
CBHW021918170626
46807CB00007B/2881
9780999040379